I0579457

A COWBOY WEDDING

Wyoming Wildflowers series
Book 7

Patricia McLinn

www.PatriciaMclinn.com/newsletter

Wyoming Wildflowers series
Wyoming Wildflowers: The Beginning (prequel)
Almost a Bride
Match Made in Wyoming
My Heart Remembers
Wyoming Wildflowers Trilogy (Books 2–4)
A New World (prequel to Jack's Heart)
Jack's Heart
Rodeo Nights (prequel to Where Love Lives)
Where Love Lives
A Cowboy Wedding
Wyoming Wildflowers Collection (Books 1–6, plus prequels)

Copyright © Patricia McLinn
ISBN: 978-1-944126-34-6
Print Edition

Dear Readers: If you encounter typos or errors in this book, please send them to me
at Patricia@patriciamclinn.com. Even with many layers of editing, mistakes can slip
through, alas. But, together, we can eradicate the nasty nuisances. Thank you!
— Patricia McLinn

The Wedding Party & Significant Others

Jack Ralston (groom)

Valerie Trimarco (bride)

Addie Trimarco (flower girl)

Dave (best man) and Matty Brennan Currick (bridesmaid), their
children Brennan, Finn
(*Almost a Bride*)

Hannah Chalmers Randall

Dax (groomsman) and Hannah Chalmers Randall, their children Sarah,
Chalmers
(*The Rancher Meets His Match/ Bardville, Wyoming*)

Mandy Chalmers

Ethan Chalmers

Paige Underwood

Cahill and Eleanor Thatcher McCrea, their son Sam
(*A New World*)

Kiernan McCrea

Felicity Roberts (Lis Robertson)—sister was Hayley Robertson

Ed and Donna Roberts Currick
(*Wyoming Wildflowers: The Beginning*)

Partial Guest List

Irene and Ted Weston

Boone and Cambria Weston Smith
(*A Stranger in the Family/ Bardville, Wyoming*)

Cal and Taylor Larsen Ruskoff, their children Cassie and Rob
(*Match Made in Wyoming*)

Shane and Lisa Currick Garrison, their daughter Alexa
(*My Heart Remembers*)

Dr. Zoe Parisi and Matt Halderman
(*Where Love Lives*)

Walker and Kalli Riley
(*Rodeo Nights*)

Hugh and Ruth Moski

Rev. Ervin Foley

The Widow Brontman

Bryan and other Slash-C ranch hands

Doc Johnson

Polly and Della from the doctor's office

Rainie Lester

Annie and John Gatchell

Brandy from the post office

Connor Malloy and son Jarrod

Other Family and Friends

Lucy Trimarco (mother of the bride)

Jimmy Trimarco (father of the bride)

Anthony and Tanya Trimarco, their kids

Bobby and Melinda Trimarco, their kids

Manuela Ruiz, The Fishwife

Trimarco cousins

Val's college roommate, friends from Gloucester, chef and former
boss, former colleague at radio station.

Thomas, Judi and Becky from the Vance Ranch
(*The Runaway Bride/ The Wedding Series*)

PROLOGUE

Donna Currick stared out to where the Big Horn Mountains lifted the western horizon toward a sky bedazzled in erratic streaks of orange, red, purple, yellow.

Valerie Trimarco started to hurry past her, bound to the barn to check on the first batch of quilts friends and neighbors had brought by. They would cover hay bales for seating during the wedding ceremony next weekend. Before that they would be hung out to air, according to the Wedding Master Schedule. But for now they were in the barn. Rain was forecast for tonight. The barn roof was tight, but still…

These quilts had been shared by dear neighbors and friends from around the Slash-C and Knighton, Wyoming. She wanted to make absolutely certain they were safe.

But something in Donna's stillness stopped her.

"Donna? Are you okay?"

The matriarch of the Slash-C smiled as she said, "I'm fine." Yet she kept staring at that horizon.

"What are you doing?"

"Just thinking, dear."

"Thinking about what?" Even as she asked, Valerie wondered at herself for pursuing this. She and Jack were getting married next weekend, friends and family would begin arriving Tuesday, and despite their determined effort to keep this wedding simple, fun, low-key, and uncomplicated, with invaluable help from Donna and her daughter-in-law Matty, myriad details—*hello? the quilts?*—kept popping up like prairie dog holes as far as she could see.

"I'm thinking about weddings. Do you ever think about weddings?" Donna asked dreamily.

Val laughed. "Yeah, you could say I think about weddings. Feels like that's all I've thought about these past few weeks. Well, weddings and Gonzo here." She patted her five months pregnant belly. "And Addie and Jack."

"Oh, I know, Val. But I mean weddings in a more general way. The big picture."

This dreamy, unfocused tone was so unlike Donna that Val was … not weirded out, because that wasn't possible with this gracious, caring, practical woman. When Donna had married Ed Currick and come to the Slash-C decades ago to start a life and a family, everyone said it was the making of the man and the ranch. Now she and Ed were enjoying retirement while their son Dave, his wife Matty, and Jack Ralston, as foreman, ran the Slash-C.

From the small house built for them on the ranch as a home base, Donna and Ed traveled as they pleased, which these days largely revolved around their grandchildren in New York, where their daughter and son-in-law lived.

A year ago, Donna had been instrumental in helping Jack and Val overcome a major hurdle to realize they truly loved each other.

Well, mostly Donna helped Jack overcome it, because he was hard-headed and stubborn. Val, on the other hand, had known they should be together long before he'd recognized it. Something she reminded him of … now and then.

With all that she owed Donna, Val mentally told the quilts they'd have to wait a minute, and asked the question she thought the older woman wanted to answer.

"What about the big picture?"

"Ah," Donna breathed out in apparent satisfaction. "Have you ever thought about how a wedding is two people, standing face to face, pledging their hearts, their lives, their futures?"

Oh, yes, she had, and if she could do that right this minute with Jack, she would. She touched her stomach. Already had.

"Beyond those two, their two families encircle them. From different backgrounds, divergent experiences, distant homes. Coming together, mingling, sharing, all to celebrate the one they already love and the one they are taking into their family."

Her family had certainly already taken Jack in during this past winter he'd spent with her in Gloucester, Massachusetts. And loved him. He had no biological relatives that he knew of. His family were the people of the Slash-C, who had already taken Val to their hearts when she arrived here unexpectedly last summer.

Donna wasn't done. "Another step from the two at the center of this circle, takes you to their friends, their communities. Wishing them well, celebrating with them."

Val smiled, thinking of all the wonderful friends she'd made in Wyoming, as well as the friends from earlier times who would be arriving next week.

"To another degree of separation," Donna continued. "Extended family, friends, community. And out to the Plus Ones, who might not know anyone at this gathering except their wedding date."

Kiernan's mystery girlfriend.

Finally—*finally*—she and Jack would get to meet her. Kiernan had clearly been head over heels for her last winter, but she and Jack and Addie had returned to Wyoming before he introduced her to anyone in Gloucester. Val had heard reports from her cousin, Eleanor, and El's husband Cahill, who was Kiernan's older brother.

Now she'd finally get to meet Felicity, The Mystery Woman herself.

And make up her own mind.

Kiernan was all grown up, and a handsome devil, yet Val felt oddly protective of the now-man who towered over her.

"All these individuals brought together, all these paths crossing that might otherwise never have crossed, all these other hearts, lives, futures that can be changed forever during the celebration of a wedding, all started by two people falling in love."

Donna turned toward Val, the vagueness gone, replaced by a smile.

"I'm so pleased that our long-time friends the Westons agreed to come for several days. It's been a long time since we've been able to spend any extended time together, between our running ranches and raising kids, and then all the traveling Ed and I have done. It's wonderful that you invited them."

"It was all Jack's doing. He got to know them through Dax and Hannah Randall. He and Dax connected over abused horses. It's too bad Cambria and Boone can't come for the whole time, but at least they'll be here for the wedding," she said of the Westons' daughter and son-in-law.

"And we're sure hoping Hannah can talk her sister and brother and his girlfriend to come, too—they're staying at the Circle CR now."

Donna put her arm around Val's shoulders. "We have you and Jack to thank for bringing Irene and Ted here. And now Dax Randall and his wife and her family. That's what I was thinking about. How weddings bring all these people together … and all that it can set in motion."

CHAPTER ONE

Circle CR Ranch
Bardville, Wyoming

"A wedding?" Ethan Chalmers repeated his older sister's words, but without her enthusiasm.

Paige sat back, quietly prepared to wait out what would come.

She'd known the Chalmers most of her life. For nearly as long she'd been in love with Ethan Chalmers.

"It'll be fun," Hannah said firmly. She was a decade older than Ethan and his twin sister, Mandy, and had taken on raising them when their parents died before the twins started high school.

Ethan showed no sign of hearing her. "Why didn't you tell us you were going to a friend's wedding? We wouldn't have come—"

"That's exactly why she didn't tell you," Mandy said.

"—out this week."

"That's why," Hannah confirmed. "You take so little time off and get out here to the ranch so seldom that I didn't want to give you any excuse to not come."

"If he weren't such a workaholic, he could come as often as I do," Mandy, said immediately. "And—

"Being responsible does not equate with being a workaholic. You might not—"

"—bring Paige because she loves it here in Wyoming, too."

He turned and looked at her in mild surprise. "Do you?"

"I do. I love the views and the air and the sky. And, most of all, I love seeing Hannah and Dax and the kids. But, about this wedding..." She looked at her boyfriend's older sister. "We don't know these people, Hannah."

Boyfriend.

Rather a strange term for this tall, broad-shouldered, handsome, grown-up man she intended to spend the rest of her life with. But maybe because she and Ethan Chalmers had started dating so young, it fit.

"I think it will be fun," Mandy said.

"As Paige said, we won't know any of the people. We'll stay here."

She looked over at him. Two reactions—both familiar and long-standing—welled up in her simultaneously.

How much she loved him.

How smart he was about most things and astonishingly dim about a few others.

For example, you'd think he'd know his twin—for that matter, both his sisters—better by now.

"Just because you're a dour grump who objects to romance because you think it doesn't fit *The Plan*—" Mandy started.

"That is inaccurate and—"

"—which is so rigid you probably have when you and Paige can kiss on a schedule, much less when you can—"

"Mandy," Hannah inserted before she got too personal.

Ethan ignored the interruptions from his sisters and continued on. "—nonsense borne of hyperbole. Hyperbole is the antithesis of logic."

"Logic? Sheesh." Mandy's expressive face twisted. "We're talking romance. A wedding. Fun. Dancing. Toasts. Watching two people be blissfully happy about starting a life together."

"I have nothing against that at the proper time. And—" He looked at Hannah. "—when it involves people I know."

"Proper time," grumbled Mandy. "Paige's biological clock will be well past its sell-by date—"

"Mixed metaphor."

"Ethan," Hannah scolded. If the twins started critiquing each other's comments, this would not only get off track fast, but it could go on forever.

"—before Ethan Scrooge over here thinks he's got sufficient piles of money to do anything. You'll end up childless, which might be a blessing for the kids of the world, except Paige would be a great mother."

"If it comes to that, we'll adopt," he said calmly.

"I wonder if Jack will adopt Addie—that's Val's little girl. Did you know that's how they met, Paige?"

She and Hannah had been doing this distract-the-twins-from-squabbling for years. "Oh, yes—how he delivered the baby in a snowstorm when her car got stuck. That's amazing."

"I know, but it wasn't until Valerie came back last summer, with Addie a toddler now, that she and Jack connected for good. Jack and Addie adore each other. When they came up to deliver a young horse he'd worked with, it was clear they're already a family, and now they'll have another one late this fall."

"She's already pregnant?" Ethan asked.

Mandy jumped in. "Oh, for heaven's sake. You know, if anyone else said that I'd accuse him of being a judgmental prig. But you're *worse.* You're disapproving because it's poor planning."

"It is. It makes far more sense to—"

Mandy threw up her hands. "Sense? It's a *baby*, Ethan. They love each other and they're having a baby together. I think it's marvelous."

"A baby needs to be housed and clothed and fed, plus a lot of needs beyond those basics. Medical bills and orthodonture and education. That all has to be provided. It all has to be planned for."

"You forgot love and understanding. Can't buy those."

He ignored Mandy's point. "A stable foundation in life and career are vital before raising a child."

"Because Hannah did *such* a lousy job of bringing us up after Mom and Dad died," Mandy shot back.

"I didn't say that."

"She scrimped and saved and managed and struggled—"

"All the more reason we should avoid that situation, since we saw what she went through. She had to struggle with difficult circumstances, fight against not having a stable foundation."

"—yet she did a great job with us because she loves us."

"She overcame obstacles. Absolutely. There is no reason, however, to repeat those obstacles when you can avoid them. And there's no reason to attend the wedding of people you don't know when you can avoid it by saying no thank you."

"That's—"

"You're being—"

"Dax?" Hannah invited her husband into the fray.

As usual, he'd stayed out of the twins' tiffs. In general, Paige agreed with that strategy, because the only thing that got them wound up more than each other was anyone—*anyone*—saying something about the other twin.

The exceptions for Dax's noninvolvement were if Hannah asked him to step in or if he thought anyone got too rough with her, in which case he stepped in, asked or not.

"You'll know people. Ted and Irene are real close with the Curricks," he said, referring to the older generation of the Westons, who owned a neighboring ranch to the Circle CR. "Don't know if Cambria and Boone will get back in time. But Ted and Irene will be there for sure. Plus some others you've met over the years of coming here to visit."

"Hah!" Mandy exulted.

The Westons had started a B&B to smooth out dips in their ranching income. It hadn't thrived until their daughter, Cambria, took it over. Cambria and her husband, who owned a successful log-building company, and their family now split time between North Carolina and Wyoming.

But before that, when Boone Dorsey Smith was courting Cambria, he'd brought his employee, Hannah Chalmers, here to Bardville, Wyoming, for a working vacation. That's when she and Dax met.

"Still," Ethan said, clearly not ready to relinquish ground, "for us to go to the wedding of your friend—"

"Not just *a friend*. Dax is in the wedding party. You should have seen him when Jack asked." Hannah grinned broadly at her husband, sitting at the head of the table with their young son, Chal, on his lap. Chal was short for Hannah's maiden name, Chalmers. Their daughter, Sarah, named for Dax's side of the family, was sitting on Ethan's lap, happily eating all the icing off his piece of cake. Dax smiled back at Hannah, who added, "He was thrilled."

"Hannah," he protested mildly.

"You were—are. Jack's a great guy. They sort of knew each other the way a lot of the ranchers sort of know each other from one county to another. But then they connected at a livestock auction a few years back when they saw someone with a starving pregnant mare and the two of them swooped in and rescued her."

Mandy looked toward Dax. "You swooped? I'd like to have seen that."

He grinned at her teasing. "Wouldn't have said swooped."

"What would you say then?" Mandy challenged him.

"More like we persuaded the guy that sending the mare to another home would be his best option."

"You made him give you the mare?"

He shrugged. "*Made him*'s too strong. Like I said—"

"Right, you persuaded him." Mandy chuckled. "Is this Jack Ralston as persuasive as you are?"

"More."

"Not more," Hannah instantly said, ceding that anyone topped her husband at anything.

Paige raised a hand to mask her smile.

Dax didn't bother to hide his. "When it comes to abused horses he sure is. And the work he does rehabilitating them is top-notch."

"He does accomplish miracles with them," Hannah acknowledged. "Cambria's using several for the bed and breakfast's trail rides."

"They must be really well trained to let those greenhorns loose on them," Mandy said.

"Mostly Cambria rides them or someone she knows is an experienced rider."

Ethan ignored Hannah's comment and said to his twin, "Hah, the greenhorn calling the greenhorn green."

"At least I ride every time I'm out here, which is a lot more often than you bother to, since you're rigid and a workaholic on top of it."

"Back to this wedding," Ethan said.

Paige bit the inside of her cheeks. Ethan knew he'd lost that round, so he'd shifted to being reasonable, organized, and above trading barbs with Mandy ... after trading barbs with her.

He continued, "Somebody needs to stay and look after the ranch, right? With Will in Australia—" Dax's first son was working on a cattle ranch there to expand his experience and see some of the world. "—and Pete Weston presumably going to the wedding—"

"Nope. He's playing in a college baseball summer league on the East Coast," Dax said of the Westons' son.

"Also, I think there's a girl," Hannah said.

"Pete Weston's caught at last?" Mandy asked with a grin.

"Regardless of the reason," Ethan persisted, "he's not available to look after things for you, either. We can stay here while you go to the wedding and we'll—"

"What? Punch a cow? Are you going to make Paige mend fence?" Mandy demanded. "Or—"

"It's all taken care of," Dax said. "A couple friends of Will's from the ranch management program at college arrive tomorrow. They've both been here before and know their way around plenty to keep an eye on things here and at the Westons' while we're gone."

"See?" Hannah said. "Everything's set. We're all invited. And you have to come. You'll like these people. We'll help with the wedding prep and the partying." She grinned. "It's going to be a great time. It's not even all that far—south of here some."

"A day trip?" Mandy asked.

Paige looked at the two sisters. That sounded like a set-up question.

"Oh, no," Hannah said immediately. "They've invited people for several days. We'll go Tuesday and come back Sunday. It's like the early ranchers used to do here. Tell them, Dax."

"People were spread out, and it took so long to travel to an event, they'd make it worthwhile by going for a few days."

"Exactly," Hannah said. "Matty says these days the problem isn't covering distances, but having time. Because everyone's so busy. She says as long as folks are making the trip, they want everyone to enjoy it for a few days."

Ethan picked up his device, a silent sign of surrender. The only one who didn't seem to recognize it as such was Ethan. "*If* we go, we'll need to know the name of the town."

"Knighton's closest to the Slash-C, but the wedding will be at the ranch."

He was typing away. "We'd get hotel rooms—"

Hannah laughed. "No you wouldn't. There's no hotel in Knighton. Or motel. Not even a B&B like the Westons'. We'll all stay at the ranches."

"Ranches? Plural?"

"They run the two family ranches together—the Curricks' Slash-C and the Brennans' Flying W, that's Matty's family ranch."

Ethan wasn't distracted from what was, for him, the main point. "We can't intrude on them like that. We'd—"

"You won't be intruding. I guarantee it. And if you don't stay where she tells you to stay you'll mess up Matty's plan.

"Wait a minute," Mandy said. "Matty's plan? But you said the bride's name is Valerie, right?"

Ah, so Mandy *had* heard about the wedding before this conversation.

Ethan didn't seem to notice, though.

"It is. Val—Valerie—Trimarco is marrying Jack Ralston, who's the foreman of the combined Flying W and Slash-C ranches. But Matty's doing some of the planning, including the sleeping arrangements, and she's a woman after you own heart, Ethan."

Mandy groaned. "The female version of The Man with the Plan? Charts? Diagrams? Minute by minute campaigns? I might have to rethink my answer. No, wait. What am I saying? I wouldn't miss it for the world. Is Dax going to be in a tuxedo? That alone would make it unmissable."

Dax groaned.

"No tuxedoes," Hannah said with a chuckle. "Though he'd carry off a tuxedo perfectly. It's going to be a casual, western affair with lots of fun before and after, in addition to the main event Saturday."

"Multiple days, staying right there, I don't think—"

Ethan's ruminations were interrupted by Hannah standing quickly. Paige and Hannah exchanged a look of perfect understanding. If Ethan made a firm decision now it would be no and it would be hard to budge him.

"What I think is it's time for these two little ones to get to bed. Chal's already asleep and Sarah's nodding off despite the sugar high courtesy of her uncle."

"Hey, I didn't—" Ethan started.

But Paige stopped him by resting her hand on his, saying, "Let's go for a walk."

Simultaneously, Hannah lifted Sarah out of his lap, then hooked a hand in Mandy's arm, saying, "Come help me with Sarah, then you can tell me what to wear." There was nothing surer to grab Mandy's attention. "Dax, if you'll bring Chal?"

"Sure thing."

As they left in opposite directions, Paige looked over her shoulder. Hannah was doing the same. Their eyes met again.

Perfect understanding.

To her surprise, Paige heard a chuckle, and realized Dax was watching both of them.

CHAPTER TWO

"Amazing how much you can see out here when the moon's shining like this, even with a few days to go to full," Ethan said.

"Mmm."

"Dax could trim expenses by not having the outside lights come on for nights like this."

"Mmm."

He started doing calculations aloud, but hadn't gotten deep into it when he slowed, stopped, then looked at her.

"Something wrong?"

"Wrong? No."

"You're quiet. Are you still feeling bad from that bout of food poisoning you had from the airport food?"

"I'm not convinced it was food poisoning. It didn't feel quite like that. But either way, I'm feeling better."

Though still rather ... *odd.*

"Then why so quiet?"

"I was thinking about how long we've known each other." More accurately, she'd been thinking about how long she'd loved Ethan Chalmers.

Sure, different kinds of love at different stages, yet love all along.

How she'd loved him in their first encounter in kindergarten was not how she'd loved him at fifteen when they thought they were grown up, and that was not how she loved him now that they were twenty-five and realizing how much was ahead of them. Different, but all love.

Even during their college years when her parents had insisted on her going to a different school so they'd see other people.

She'd known it wouldn't change her feelings. But Ethan *had* pulled away from her. Living up to what her parents wanted more than she ever had.

Until the summer before the second year of his masters program and her second year of teaching.

She'd been on a stretch of moving walkway in the Charlotte airport, going to a flight for a teaching conference. He'd been coming the opposite direction with Mandy, returning—as she now knew—from a visit here at the Circle CR.

He'd stopped dead on the walkway, much to the consternation of other travelers. That's when she'd seen him.

As the walkways carried them past each other, he came back to life, telling her to wait for him to get to the end of his walkway and he'd catch up with her.

Mandy shoved him. "Don't be such a rule-follower."

He'd glanced at his sister, ordered her to take his bag, then vaulted over the twin barriers dividing the two walkways and, with the cooperation of a few sympathetic travelers, caught up with her.

They'd talked until she had to board or miss her flight.

He'd picked her up from the airport on her return, and they hadn't been apart since.

Now, he released her hand and put his arm around her shoulders, drawing her snug against his side. Her arm went around his waist, hooking through a loop on his jeans. It was a familiar, a comfortable, a beloved way for them to stand or walk together.

He kissed the top of her head. "We're going to have decades together."

A pain spasmed through her. Not horrible. In fact, quite familiar, though this wasn't the right time for its usual cause.

Must be a carryover from whatever had upset her stomach during their trip.

Planning the Wedding:
The Overall Plan

"It's going to be the simplest wedding ever. Family and friends there. That's all. Simple and casual."

Val sat with Matty and Donna on the back porch of the Slash-C ranch house, enjoying a sunny spring day, while Jack leaned against the pole, half-smiling.

"What other decisions have you made?" Matty asked.

"We won't take a honeymoon."

"No honeymoon?" Matty repeated.

"Well, not right away. Not until after roundup, after the baby, after Christmas. But before calving season. Maybe February."

"What about everything else?"

"What do you mean everything else? It's going to be really simple and casual. Just family and friends."

"But—"

Donna cut off her daughter-in-law's objection. "Okay, that's clear—simple and casual. And family and friends tell us who. Now the where and when. I suggest you do it here."

"Oh, but my mother and my cousin, El—"

Matty interrupted. "Will have you back in Massachusetts for when the baby's born. Besides, they need to come here and see your other home."

Valerie looked at Jack. "What do you think?"

"Wherever you'll marry me is fine with me."

She faked a grimace. "You're a big help."

"Here's something for you both to consider." Donna looked

so mild that Valerie had a feeling she was about to play her ace. "If you get married in Gloucester, either Val and Addie would certainly have to go back there for a good chunk of time while Jack's working here, or you'd have to wait until you're there this winter. Although planning a wedding with a brand new baby, plus the potential for travel problems in the winter for out of town guests, like all of us from Wyoming, could complicate issues."

Val eyed the older woman. They both knew that had caught Jack's attention. The part where he was in Wyoming while she and Addie were in Gloucester hadn't gone over any better with him than the idea of delaying.

"Those are good points, Val," he said. "We can get married right away here, but we'd have to wait months and months to do it in Gloucester."

"Unless—" Donna gave a final tap to the nails in the coffin of a Gloucester wedding with a benign smile. "—Val goes back there for an extended time. Addie, too, of course."

Jack straightened from the pole. "No. You asked what I think, Val, and I think we should get married here. Right away."

Donna reached up and patted his arm. "*Right away* might be a little optimistic, dear, but I think you've made an excellent decision."

"Now that that's settled," Matty said, "we need to make a list…"

CHAPTER THREE

After lunch the next day, Ethan dropped down to the floor at little Sarah's request that he look at her toy horses. There was a roundup going on.

They'd been too busy this morning with a ride out to move cattle to fresh grazing to renew the discussion about the wedding, especially since she and Ethan had taken a pickup with the kids, while the others were on horseback.

Now that everyone else had cleaned the table, Paige gave it a final wipe.

"Hannah," she said quietly, stopping her from walking past. "Do you want me to try to talk to Ethan about going to the wedding?"

A flicker of something crossed Hannah's face, then was gone. She patted Paige's shoulder. "Thank you, but no. We'll work it out. One way or another."

Hannah picked up a stack of clean laundry, stepped over the horse roundup, and disappeared down the hallway.

Paige watched Ethan with his young niece, who was earnestly explaining that Polly the pony was the leader of the horses, so needed to be rounded up first.

He truly was good with kids.

He should have children of his own.

She pushed the thought aside. She wouldn't borrow trouble.

Besides, Ethan had a plan.

Plans were important to him. Necessary.

Yet, for this little girl and her brother, she knew he would throw out every plan, spreadsheet, list in the universe.

Paige smiled, though tears stung her eyes.

She stood. "I'm going to take a nap."

Ethan looked around. "You're what?"

"Going to take a nap."

"All right, dear," Hannah said, returning to the room. "We'll try to hold the noise down."

"No need. Feels like I could fall asleep standing up right here."

Ethan was still staring. "You never take naps."

"We're on vacation. This seems like a good time to start."

Mandy plunked down next to Paige on the front porch steps, shaded by an overhang from the strong, slanting late afternoon sun.

Mandy looked across to where Dax was working on a horse's hooves, while Ethan sat on the fence nearby. "I bet Dax is trying to talk some sense into Ethan about going to the wedding."

Paige had been watching the two men, thinking about how unlikely it was that they had ever been brought together into a family, yet how well they got along … in an understated, man-bonding kind of way.

It was too bad Will wasn't here. He had a way of bringing out a younger, less responsible side of Ethan.

"Maybe Dax'll get through to him," Mandy said. "Have you and Ethan talked about it?"

"No."

"He's such a downer. Why can't he say, *Yes, of course, we'll go to the wedding you're looking forward to, Hannah?*"

"He needs time to absorb the change in plans."

"My brother. The man with the plan."

"It's one of the things I love about him."

Mandy looked at her. "I know. I'll never understand it."

Paige laughed. She also loved Mandy. How could she not? The bond between brother and sister could have been used to pushed away any outsider. Instead, from the first, Ethan's twin sister had opened that twinness, making room for Paige. "Why? I'm an organized person, too."

"Yeah, *now* you are. What choice have you had being with Ethan all the time? It was bound to rub off on you."

"Didn't rub off on you."

She perked up. "That's true. So there's at least one member in the resistance to The Plan."

"Don't exaggerate, Mandy. You make it sound like he's a dictator."

"Isn't he? It's not only plans, it's plans clad in iron. And doesn't that master plan of his dictate how your whole life is going to be, when you'll buy a house, where, what kind, with how much down payment. Not to mention when you're going to get married, when you're going to have kids—all because it's practical?"

"It *is* practical."

Mandy's hands came up in a *See? See what I'm saying?* gesture.

"Practical is not always bad," she said gently. "If you'd let him look at your business setup—"

"We're talking about Ethan."

Mandy's Do Not Trespass sign was large, neon, and flashing.

"Okay." Paige gave her a level look. "For now."

Mandy blinked first, silently acknowledging that though this topic was being dropped now, it would be addressed again.

With that mutually understood acknowledgment, Paige relented and returned to the topic Mandy wanted to discuss. "He needs to plan, Mandy. You know that as well as anybody could."

"I might know it, but I don't understand it. You'd think that Mom and Dad's death would make him want to *live*, not create spreadsheets."

"He does want to live—he *does* live—just not the way you do. Did his natural tendency toward responsibility and planning get exaggerated? Yes. Just as your natural tendency toward seizing the day and letting tomorrow take care of itself deepened and widened. I wish the two of you would talk—*really* talk. About everything. Especially about your parents."

"Nothing to talk about." Mandy stood. "See you later."

The comfortable silences between Ethan and Dax had been broken now and then with comments about the weather, the horse, the baseball standings, and Will's adventures in Australia.

Then Dax said, out of nowhere, "Hannah wants you to come. The wedding, I mean. Jack and Val's wedding at the Slash-C."

Ethan chuckled. "Uh-huh. Hannah wants it, so that's the end of it for you, but not necessarily for me or—"

"She wants to spend as much time as possible with you. She misses you and Paige and Mandy."

"We miss her, too." He cleared his throat. "But we also know how happy she is here. With you. With the kids. Having this family and home."

Dax looked up. Their look held for a moment, then broke.

It was one of the things he liked about his brother-in-law. You knew where you stood with him, without a lot of discussion.

What he liked more, though, was how Dax loved and treated Hannah. Couldn't ask for better.

Hannah had tried to shield him and Mandy from her struggles when she took on raising them. But he'd seen them.

She did a great job with us because she loves us.

Mandy might choose to view it all as some romantic ideal of focusing on love and small pleasures in the face of not enough money or hours in the day to cover the necessities, like some scene in an animated movie with birds that trilled and flitted around the heroine while she picked berries because there's no food in the larder.

He knew better. He'd seen the scrimping, saving, and struggling.

Hannah with her head in her hands, the computer showing figures that weren't adding up, even when she'd tried re-adding on a legal pad, while he'd watched, unseen from the stairway after she thought he and Mandy were asleep.

Hannah had told them that their parents' insurance would let them keep the house. And their college educations were taken care of, because their parents had put money away for that.

What she didn't say but he knew was that without both their parents' incomes living expenses for the four years before they started college all fell on her shoulders.

Working for Boone Dorsey Smith's company had helped that a lot.

Still, Ethan had seen her weariness and worry.

He'd also seen her sorrow.

That jackass Richard had told her not even two weeks after the funeral that he couldn't handle a couple of teenagers hanging on to her apron strings forevermore because her parents crashed their plane. There were programs that could handle them and he'd allow a reasonable time for her to settle them in one, but she had to make the decision right then. Their marriage or *those kids*.

He and Mandy had both been listening on the stairs that time. Not looking at each other.

Hannah's voice had come fast and firm. "Good-bye, Richard."

That had been no great loss—he'd been a jerk—but it had hurt Hannah.

Somewhere in that first year, Ethan had pledged to himself that he'd make it easier on her. He'd streamlined his activities. He'd ruthlessly organized the house from top to bottom—what had been cheerful chaos with both their parents on hand to sort it out had become a swamp for Hannah to try to get through. He'd gotten rid of any clothes that needed special care, then taught himself to do laundry and cook. He'd nagged and challenged Mandy into doing the same. In fairness, she hadn't resisted all that much, especially the cooking part.

She'd also been able to do something he couldn't—make Hannah laugh.

So he went with his strengths.

He'd started creating plans to keep it all on track, to keep the burden of carrying on from threatening to crush Hannah or anyone else he was connected to. He couldn't guarantee nothing would happen to him, not any more than his parents had been able to guarantee they wouldn't crash the small plane they'd been flying that day, but he could set things up so that no matter what, those he loved would be okay.

"So?" Dax asked.

Oh, right. His brother-in-law had asked about going to that wedding near Knighton, Wyoming. "I'll talk with Paige."

Dax coughed. It wasn't much of a disguise for a chuckle.

"What do you think she'll say?" he asked.

Ethan sighed. "That we're going to a wedding."

Planning the Wedding:
The Venue

After deciding the wedding would be in Wyoming, Jack went to the ranch office, while Val, Matty, and Donna remained on the porch.

Val said, "So I suppose the first thing to figure out is where, specifically, and when. Do you think the church in town would let us use their basement for a non-denominational wedding? Otherwise it means Jefferson, and that would be okay, but having it in Knighton would be easier for people here."

"When I said hold the wedding here, I meant the Slash-C," Donna said.

"Of course, you'll be married here at the ranch," Matty agreed.

"But…But that would be so much work for you."

"Not at all." Donna smiled at her daughter-in-law. "Especially not if you let Matty run things."

"That's right. I've got it down to a science. With Lisa and Shane's wedding, and Donna and Ed's anniversary party and—"

Donna chuckled. "And more other events than she can remember."

"That's true. But it's been a while since we've had a big party—too long." Apparently interpreting Val's expression and open mouth correctly, she added, "A really big *casual* and *simple* party. Now, let's talk dates."

Calendars were consulted, several family members were texted, which narrowed it down to two possibilities in August.

Val picked one.

"Next major question—inside or outside?"

"Oh, outside if we can. But if it rains…"

"We'll clean out the barn and use that as backup. But we'll plan on outside. The patio for dinner, then dancing after. Okay?"

"That's wonderful about the patio for dancing, but we said simple. Really, really simple. Low-key. I don't think dinner… I mean a complete dinner would be—"

"Very easy. We'll talk about the details of the menu later, but if you're firm about casual and simple, we can do a sort of cookout. Steaks and grilled vegetables, then fruit salad and other stuff." She was taking notes as she spoke. "Burgers for the kids."

"Addie will be ecstatic," Val admitted.

"Now, the next question—" Matty stood and called out "Jack! Jack, c'mon over here."

He and Bryan had just come out of the office. He nodded, sending Bryan on his way, then came directly to them. "You okay?" he asked Val.

"I'm fine." She reached up and he took her hand. "But wait until you hear all this."

Matty rattled off all the plans she had come up with, including pushing up construction on the three small log houses already planned. "Good thing we're working with Boone's company. I'm sure he'll help us make sure they all get done in time."

Jack looked shellshocked.

Until she wrapped up with, "What do you want for your wedding cake?"

That he answered immediately, "Val's brownies."

Val looked up at him. "You can't have brownies, even Trimarco brownies, as a wedding cake."

Matty chuckled, taking notes. "Sure he can. What about all the rest?"

"It's real nice of you to offer the Slash-C, but it's up to Val."

"Oh, good," Matty said, "because we've already worn her down."

Val laughed. "If Jack's okay with it, we'd be honored and delighted to be married here at the Slash-C."

CHAPTER FOUR

TUESDAY

Slash-C Ranch
Knighton, Wyoming

The barn cleanup was already done.

The horses were out to pastures for the season. They'd removed all machinery and unnecessary paraphernalia. Bryan had been close to becoming a permanent prune with all the pressure washing inside and out he'd done. Around the foundation, they'd filled in and covered up with woodchips.

That was only the beginning.

They scrubbed the back porch and patio to operating room standards. They cleaned all the houses and buildings where people would stay, both at the Slash-C and the Flying W, Matty's family ranch, which adjoined the Slash-C and was run in tandem with it.

Val had protested at all this work, but the Curricks insisted they were all due for a good cleaning anyway.

Big barrels were rolled up on either side of the barn doors, soil added, and planted with flowers. More were planted around all the buildings.

Until Ed Currick grumbled one day that he feared that if he stood still too long he'd have flowers planted around him.

And then things started to arrive.

Trucks, four-wheel-drives, and even an occasional car showed up with chairs, tables, linens, plates, quilts, glasses, vases, silverware, two major grills, two extra refrigerators, and more that Val couldn't keep up with.

"How am I ever going to thank everyone?" she asked Matty.

"No need. They're thanking you for what you've done."

"What have I done?"

"You've made Jack happy."

Planning the Wedding:
The Wedding Party

They sat, as they often did at the end of a day, on the porch steps. Jack on the top step, with Val between his legs on the next step down, then Addie between Val's legs on the step below that.

"Addie?"

"Uh-huh."

"You know Jack and I are getting married."

"Uh-huh. Does that mean I call you Daddy Jack?"

Jack reached past Val and tousled Addie's hair. "You call me whatever you want. And you can change your mind as time goes on."

"Okay."

"Would you like to be in our wedding?" Val asked.

"Sure. What does that mean?"

"Well, you'd be with us standing up in front of the people who come to share our wedding. You'd be what's called the flower girl."

"What's that?"

"It's the very important girl who walks in front of the bride and tosses flower petals down in front of her."

Addie twisted around to look up at her mother. "You mean they tear apart the flowers? Why?"

"That's a good question. It's a tradition from a long, long time ago."

"Huh. Sounds weird. People shouldn't tear apart flowers."

It was Val's turn to twist around and look up. Jack smiled and gave the slightest shrug. "Up to you."

Val faced her daughter. "You have a good point, Addie. We'll think about that. But as long as we don't tear up flowers will you be my flower girl?"

"Sure. What's Brennan gonna be?"

Val blinked at her. "Brennan?"

Jack stepped in. "We'll think of something good for him to do, too. Okay, Addie?"

"Okay, Daddy Jack. Oh, look, Storm is coming to say hi." She jumped off the step and ran to the fence where the horse was nickering and nodding his head as if urging the child to come say hello.

They both watched as she reached the corral fence, then climbed up on the bottom rail.

"So far, so good," Jack said. Unlike the previous year, Addie had been perfect about the rule to stay on her own side of the fence unless she had a grownup with her.

Val shifted sideways on the step, leaning her back against his left knee, and looked at him. "How do you feel about being called Daddy Jack?" His grin answered that one. She tsked. "She could have called you Godzilla and you'd've been fine with it. I hope you like living wrapped around Addison Rose's little finger."

"Hers and yours and the one to come," he said with a gentle

stroke of his large hand over her belly.

She tsked again, but her grin belied it.

"So, the flower girl who won't throw flowers is set and we've gained Brennan. Now for the rest of the wedding party."

"El?" he asked.

"Absolutely. Matron of honor. Best man?"

"Thought I'd ask Dave."

She nodded. "Do you mind if I ask one more? Matty. It would mean you'd need to ask someone else, too. Is that okay?"

"Yeah."

"You're going to ask Dax Randall?"

"How'd you know?"

"Part of your network for abused horses. Sort of an equine underground railroad. And his and Hannah's Circle CR Ranch is one of the stops."

He made a sound of amusement. "Hadn't thought of it like that. But, yeah, Dax has brought a few horses in. He's also helped place a number of them after."

After was after Jack worked his magic on them. Magic, that is, if magic consisted of unending consistency and patience. With a big dollop of seeing the world through the eyes of each individual abused horse.

"Great. I like him and Hannah. They have a cool story, too. Hannah working for Boone Dorsey Smith in North Carolina and Dax with a ranch here. Seems like they'd never meet, but then Boone meets Ted and Irene Weston's daughter, Cambria, and he has Hannah come here for a two-week working visit. And now Hannah and Dax are married and have Sarah and

Chalmers."

He kissed the top of her head again. "How you remember all that, I'll never understand."

"I remember because they're important to you. Hey, what do you know? As long as everybody says yes, we've got our wedding party set."

The Circle CR Ranch group drove down in a caravan with Irene and Ted Weston.

Ethan and Paige were in the rental car, bringing up the rear behind the Westons' truck and Dax and Hannah's truck, which also held Mandy and the kids.

"Wow, this is quite a set-up," Ethan said as they followed the ranch road around the low-slung Slash-C home ranch to a lineup of small houses in a semicircle on one side, closer to the house, and the more usual ranch buildings opposite them, near the barn.

Irene had told them when they all stopped for lunch on the road that the Curricks had used Boone's log building company to add a foreman's house and small guest houses to the Slash-C this spring, one of them for the family of Lisa Currick Garrison and her husband, Shane. Not only did they come to visit frequently, but Lisa owned a share of the ranch.

"Wouldn't mind having our own guesthouse at Hannah and Dax's," Ethan said now. "Where we could get away from it all. Have some privacy."

Paige laughed at him. "And miss being awakened by Sarah patting your cheek and asking, 'Are you awake, Unca Et-an, are you awake?' Not a chance."

He grinned. "Maybe I would miss that a little."

They pulled up beside where the trucks had parked. As they all got out, a gray-haired couple came out of what appeared to be the most established of the small houses with huge smiles and waves. Both wore jeans, boots, plain shirts, and cowboy hats, yet the thought flashed through Paige that these were people who could wear anything, handle any situation, be at ease anywhere.

A young man was crossing the open area at the center of the compound. The older man on the porch called out something Paige didn't hear and the younger man turned and took off at a lope.

The Westons and the couple from the house—had to be Donna and Ed Currick—walked toward each other quickly.

Paige hung back, not wanting to intrude on their reunion. She realized all the others from their caravan were doing the same. Though the only reason Sarah did was because Hannah held her hand.

The women threw their arms open wide to hug tight and long. The men approached each other with extended hands, meeting in a shake that started at arm's length, but immediately closed into a man hug, with quick, hard thumps on their backs. Then Donna and Ted hugged, while Irene and Ed did the same.

All of their eyes were moist and all of them wore smiles.

The same was true for all of the members of their audience.

Vicariously, Paige experienced a surge of affection and warmth and respect and shared memories. It was a potent and irreplaceable mix.

She felt Ethan's hand come around hers and she squeezed back at the same time she touched Mandy's shoulder. Mandy half turned to her with a misty-eyed smile.

"…Cambria and Boone and the kids?" Donna was asking.

"Will be here Saturday for the wedding," Irene said. "But not before, I'm afraid. They're coming in from a franchise launch Boone did in Michigan. But you know some of these folks and let me introduce the others."

Irene opened the circle by waving the others forward.

"Dax, Hannah, how wonderful to see you," Donna said with her warm smile, while Ed Currick pumped Dax's hand and hugged Hannah.

"And this must be Chalmers and Sarah."

Chal waved from his father's arms, while Sarah turned suddenly and uncharacteristically shy, stepping behind her mother.

Donna scootched down. "Hi, Sarah. We have some girls and boys around here, too. We'll introduce you to them soon. And you'll all get to play together the next few days. Would you like that?"

"I guess. Are you a bride?"

A few chuckles came, but Donna remained focused on the girl, smiling only slightly. "No. I've been married a long, long time, which is a wonderful thing. You'll meet the bride soon. Her name is Valerie. Now, I understand you have some more people here who are special to you. Part of your family who come from North Carolina?"

Sarah brightened. "Uncle Et-an. Aunt Paige. Aunt Mandy."

"Exactly. I'm going to meet them now, the way you're going to meet new friends your age soon." She stood, leaving the little girl comfortable and eager to make new friends.

Irene, smiling widely, said, "Donna and Ed, I'd like you to meet Hannah's sister Mandy and her brother Ethan and his fiancée, Paige."

"We're delighted to finally meet you. We've heard so much about you from Dax and Hannah and Irene and Ted."

Donna Currick looked like a sweet lady with her gray hair, but she gave killer hugs. And Ed Currick was no slouch in that department, either.

As the conversation widened, Paige found herself standing beside Donna Currick, with Irene and Hannah nearby.

Donna put a hand on her wrist and asked quietly, "Are you all right, Paige?"

"All right? Yes. Of course. Why?"

"You're adjusting the strap on that shoulder bag like it might be bothering you. Does it hurt?"

"No. I mean, I haven't been aware of it."

"You kept shifting it around at lunch, too," Hannah said abruptly.

"I did?"

"It's probably too heavy," Ethan said with a chuckle. "I went to pick it up and it nearly brought me to my knees. You could outfit a small country with what she carries."

She made a face at Ethan, then grinned, and admitted, "I do carry a lot. I should be used to it. Don't know why it would be bothering me today. Maybe my shoulder is sore for some reason."

She caught a look between Donna and Irene that she didn't understand, but all Donna said was, "That might be it."

Hannah opened her mouth, then closed it, directing a strange look at her.

It seemed a lot of fuss over her shifting the strap of her shoulder bag more frequently than usual. Or was *she* making too much of their kindness in expressing concern that her shoulder might be sore?

There was no time to consider it further, because two young women came hurrying up, one taller and wearing a braid down her back, the other shorter and with masses of dark hair.

"Irene!" called out the taller one.

They started the hug line with the older generation, then ended with Ethan and her.

As the taller one hugged Ethan, saying only, "I'm Matty," the shorter one said, "And you're Ethan, who is Hannah's brother, right? And this must be Paige, who's been part of the family since fifth grade and the science project you two did together. You got assigned him as a partner because you were late to school that Monday because your family's car was wrecked when you went to your cousin's wedding in Raleigh."

Paige emerged from her turn to be hugged by Matty Brennan Currick, Donna's daughter-in-law, and stared at the dark-haired woman, who had to be Valerie Trimarco, the bride.

"How on earth do you know all that?" she asked.

Valerie grinned. "I listen."

"She also has this big, convoluted family that she keeps track of. She's been trained since childhood as a family-ties savant." Matty stepped back and let Val in for hugs.

"That's true. And you'll meet a bunch of them this weekend. My cousin Eleanor's in the wedding—she's the exception to the family rule. She's dependable and responsible and thinks before she speaks. But the rest of them will be roaming wild, so watch out."

"Now, Valerie, no exaggerations," Donna said. "They are wonderful, warm, welcoming—"

"And wacky," Val slipped in.

"Thank heavens," Matty said. "They'll fit right in."

"Speaking of fitting in, where are you going to fit everyone?" Hannah asked.

"Oh, that's easy," Matty said. "Irene and Ted have the guest room in Donna and Ed's place. We're putting all you Circle CR folks in Lisa and Shane's house, two bedrooms and two baths in the main part, then a bedroom and bath that has its own entry, but also can connect to inside—we thought Ethan and Paige in there. Cambria and Boone can have the pullout in the living room Saturday night, since kids will be in sleeping bags in the main house."

"If they're not dancing all night," Donna said with a smile.

"I'm so glad they're coming," Val added. "I know how much Jack's enjoyed them since Dax first arranged for them to take some of the reformed rescue horses."

"Works out great for us," Ted said.

"And there might be a new one soon. Walker Riley's bringing in a horse he says needs Jack's help." Val shrugged. "We said no wedding presents, but we can't refuse this one."

"But what about Lisa and Shane's family? With us in their house, where will they stay?" Hannah asked.

"They'll be with us in the main house," Matty said. "Shane's parents and one of Taylor's brothers and his wife will stay with Taylor and Cal at their place—they all are fond of Jack and didn't want to miss this. Eleanor and Cahill and Kiernan and Felicity, when she comes, will have the two-bedroom spare house—first ones to stay in it. Boone's building company finished it just in time. That way the wedding party is all here on the home ranch."

"That," Val said in a teasingly ominous tone, "means the Trimarco clan will take over the Flying W—the main house and the foreman's cottage. It will never be the same. Probably have a permanent mark of Massachusetts on it."

Matty picked up. "Plus three of Val's friends from Gloucester—"

"Two since kindergarten and then Manuela Ruiz, the wonderful woman who now runs the restaurant El and I started a few years back," Val said, continuing the rapid back and forth with her brides-maid.

"—will stay with Hugh and Ruth Moski in town. Two more—"

"College roommate and a friend from when I worked in radio."

"—are staying in the apartment the Moskis rent out, which is for-tunately empty at the moment."

"I couldn't believe it, but a chef I worked with is also coming, though he insisted on staying in the next county south, where he can get a chain motel, and making the drive. That's what a couple of my cousins are doing, too. Then they're going to travel around Wyoming a while."

"Walker and Kalli Riley are coming with their family, but they'll be in their posh trailer, staying with Zoe Parisi and Matt Halderman at his little ranch."

"And Jack's friends from when he first came to Wyoming are driving up Saturday and will stay over in their camper that night to be here for the brunch Sunday."

"Then all the people from Knighton, of course."

"My, oh, my. I thought you said this was going to be a small wed-ding," Irene teased.

"I know. It just kept growing and Matty—"

Whatever else Val intended to say was silenced by Matty's firm interruption. "It *is*—small and simple and easy. Guaranteed."

CHAPTER FIVE

When everyone's laughter died down, Irene said, "Valerie, I think I have your siblings, their spouses, and children all straight from Donna—"

Val looked between the two old friends. "You do? Wow."

"—but tell me again about the gorgeous young Irishman that Donna has promised is coming and how he's related to you."

Val gave a fake groan. "Oh, no. Donna, you, too? I thought there'd be at least one female who resisted Kiernan's charms."

"I simply reported the facts. And the fact is that when we came to visit you last winter in Gloucester and met both Cahill and Kiernan, I immediately fell for them. Of course, Cahill is devoted to your cousin, Eleanor, but Kiernan … ah, Kiernan is single."

Ed Currick cleared his throat. "But *you're* not single. In case that slipped your mind."

Donna beamed a smile at him that said it never had, never would slip her mind. It made Paige want to sigh aloud in satisfaction.

"No dear," Donna said with false submission and a twinkling grin. "It didn't slip my mind." Then she nudged Irene. "Wait until you see him. And hear him."

"Don't be letting him hear you say things like that," Val warned. "He's had far too much evidence already that women fall at his feet. Here's how he fits in. My cousin, Eleanor, who I mentioned before, is going to be my matron of honor, married and fell in love with—"

"You mean fell in love with and married," said Matty.

"No, but I'll let them tell their story if they choose. Anyway, Eleanor and Cahill—that's Aidan Padraic Cahill McCrea, but he goes by Cahill—got married and opened an inn in Gloucester. Kiernan is

Cahill's younger brother. Kiernan came over here from Ireland for college, and with both her sons here, their mother came, too, though their mom is missing the wedding because she's back in Ireland helping her sister who's having surgery this week. They've all settled in Gloucester. Well, Kiernan's in Boston. Though as for settled… Well, we'll see."

"Oh, you can't leave it hanging like that," Mandy protested.

Val laughed. "Okay, okay, but don't let on that I've told you or he'll skin me. Worse, he'll stop babysitting for Addie—that's our daughter—and she's wild about him. Kiernan McCrea has been breaking hearts left and right since he stepped foot in this country— probably back in Ireland, too, but I wasn't there to witness that. I don't know any details and it's not fair to guess. But I'm not guessing about since he arrived here. I saw it time after time. He wasn't mean or misleading, but girl after girl, then woman after woman were almost instantly ready to be serious. Not Kiernan. He was playing the field so well and so long he could start for the Red Sox. And then it happened."

She drew in a deep breath, looking around at her audience, making sure she had their full attention.

"He met someone who didn't fall at his feet. Who didn't want to get serious. Who made him work to win her. I suppose he must have encountered *some* other women who didn't immediately fall for him before this, but I don't know of a single one he actually pursued. This one's different. Has been from the time they met last fall. We started noticing him being more distracted—and not juggling a dozen dates— around New Years. By March we knew he was really, truly, and completely smitten."

"Oh, no," Irene said. They all looked at her in varying degrees of surprise. "He's taken? I quite had my heart set on him for Mandy."

Mandy colored up, but her "Irene, that's crazy," was good-natured.

"Is it serious?" Paige got a grateful look from Mandy for her distracting question.

"It must be serious, more serious than I've ever known him to be, because—" Val paused dramatically. "—he's bringing her to the wedding."

That drew a number of "ohs" from the females in the group, though the males seemed unmoved.

"Though he's coming in earlier, along with Eleanor and Cahill, later today, and she'll come in Thursday."

"What's she like?" Paige asked, keeping the spotlight off Mandy.

"I don't know. I haven't met her. He didn't persuade her to come to Gloucester to meet the family until after Jack and Addie and I were back here for calving season this spring. Little did she know that we're the easy-going ones who've been on her side all along. Poor thing, meeting Kiernan's mother, my parents, all my siblings, not to mention Cahill and El all at once."

"Do they like her?" Irene asked.

Hannah chuckled. "Irene, you sound like you hope they might not."

"Well, I haven't entirely given up the idea of matching him with Mandy."

"Sorry, Irene," Val said. "Everybody says she's very nice. Quiet, a little reserved, but it's hard not to be around my family. Oh, and everybody says how beautiful her eyes are—a beautiful blue color. Although El says—"

Paige had watched as a pair of men in jeans, boots, working shirts, and cowboy hats had come up behind Val without her noticing them.

Now, one put his hands on Val's shoulders and cleared his throat loudly.

Val spun around, already smiling, put her arms around him and hugged. "Jack. Come meet everybody. Well, except Dax and Hannah, of course, because you know them already. And you know Ted and Irene, right?"

Before Jack could answer, the other new arrival said plaintively, "What about me?"

Matty gave him a nudge. "Jack and Val are the stars this weekend, Dave. Get used to being a supporting actor."

Jack looked slightly taken aback, but Val chuckled as she said, "Everybody, that's Matty's husband, Dave—"

He groaned, laying it on thick, "Is that my only identity these days?"

"No, you're also the father of my children," Matty said immediately.

"And this," Val continued, undeterred. "Is Jack. Jack Ralston."

Paige thought Val said it as if introducing a member of royalty. Possibly one destined for sainthood. And the way they looked at each other…

"And Jack, this is…" Paige didn't know how he could possibly keep up with his bride-to-be's rapid-fire introductions, interspersed with history, connections, and side issues, but he seemed to take it all in stride. Shaking hands with each of them with a reserved smile, but a firm handshake.

At the end, he said, "Val, it's about time to leave for the airport to pick up El and Cahill and Kiernan."

"Is it? Already?" She looked at her watch. "It is. Great. I can't wait until you all meet each other. You know tonight we're going in to Jefferson for dinner. After tonight we'll be such a big group, we'd swamp any of the local restaurants, so we'll have the rest of our meals here at the ranch. Tomorrow is to relax and look around. Then Thursday hits high gear. All volunteers help with the food prep or the setup outside. Plus a special surprise before dinner. Then, after dinner, there are line dancing lessons for us Easterners. On Friday—"

"Eleanor and Cahill and Kiernan will still be at the airport because we haven't picked them up yet," Jack said dryly. "Let's go, General Trimarco."

"Okay, okay. Donna will you fill them in?"

She started to back away, then darted back and put her arms around Irene.

Paige heard her say softly, "Thank you so much for coming, you've made Donna and Ed so happy."

As Val and Jack walked away, he said something to her that Paige didn't catch, but she did hear a snatch of Val's reply, which included, "…you know El's concerned…"

Planning the Wedding:

The Reception

"What do you want in the reception?"

"Simple, casual—"

"And easy," Matty finished Val's sentence. "I've heard that somewhere before."

Val laughed. "I know, but that's truly what we want—to spend time with the people who come. Uh-oh, what's that glint in your eye?"

"Do you trust me?"

"How could I not with all you're doing?"

"Good. Did you ever hear about the surprise reception Dave and the rest of Knighton threw for us?"

"After you were married at the courthouse in Jefferson. I know, but that was in the church basement."

Matty waved a hand. "Immaterial. The point is, will you let me throw the surprise reception this time? Not a complete surprise, of course, since you know it's happening and you'll be involved with the menu, but some surprises. If you'll let me handle the rest?"

"Okay," Val said slowly, then more decisively, "Okay. Surprise reception it is."

CHAPTER SIX

Val looked up and down the long table and sighed with happiness.

Not only did Eleanor, Cahill, their son Sam, and Kiernan represent the beginning of the arrival of her loved ones from Gloucester—*their* loved ones, hers and Jack's because they all loved him, too—but to have Jack's friend Dax Randall and his family here, along with Donna and Ed's dear friends…

The older Curricks and the Westons were thoroughly enjoying each other at the other end of the table.

Eleanor was chatting with Hannah and that sweet Paige Underwood, who was engaged to Ethan Chalmers. Ethan and Kiernan had hit it off and were talking sports. Dax, Cahill, Dave, and Matty were trading stories about their businesses. Mandy Chalmers was charming the Randall and Currick kids, along with Addie.

This was what Donna had been talking about—about how weddings brought together people who might otherwise never have met.

It was perfect. Absolutely perfectly. Exactly what she'd hoped for.

Jack's hand covered hers under the table.

She looked at him and saw the smile in his eyes. "Don't start crying again," he warned.

"Sometimes it's just too good not to cry."

"What if I start bawling with you?"

She chuckled. "That would make me cry even more."

"Nope. Can't have that."

She sighed again. "You better prepare yourself, Jack. I'll probably cry through the whole wedding. These hormones have got me on permanent flood mode. I might wash out the whole thing and I'll float away."

He threaded his fingers through hers. "No you won't. I'll fill sand-bags from here to kingdom come and keep you safe."

They looked into each other's eyes and smiled.

"Val?"

Donna's soft call came from out of the dark as Val left the lighted porch and started from the Slash-C main house to the little house that had been built for Jack and her and their family.

With her eyes adjusting, Val saw it wasn't totally dark. There was a flickering glow from right where Donna and Ed's front porch should be.

She headed for that and soon saw Donna and Irene sitting on the rockers there with a candle burning in a lantern between them.

"Were you and Matty still working?" Donna asked as Val came up the steps.

"Going over some final details."

"Doubt they'll be the last ones," Donna said. "Your ears should have been burning, by the way. We've been sitting here since the two old fogies we're married to went to bed, having a fine time talking about you and Jack."

"Old fogies?" Val repeated with delight. "Wait until I tell Ed."

Irene chuckled. "We were talking about how happy you and Jack are and the wonderful transformation in him. It's … it's dazzling. Such a good man and to see him happy now…"

She couldn't have said anything better to Val's mind.

And then Irene added, "I very much enjoyed spending time with your cousin, Eleanor, and her husband, Cahill. They honored me by telling me a bit about how they came together."

Val grinned. "You mean Cahill told you."

Irene smiled. "Eleanor did add a few details, but, yes, he was the primary storyteller."

"I'm so glad Eleanor let him in to her heart," she said impulsively. "She was too *careful* and guarded. It took someone as wonderful as Cahill to break through to her and even then, I wondered…"

Irene nodded with an amused glint in her eyes. "I understand. I've known young women like that."

"I just hope Kiernan is as lucky as Cahill and El."

"Whyever shouldn't he be? Your Kiernan's not the lady-killer your description had me expecting."

"Ah, you saw it, too." Donna sounded entirely satisfied.

"What are you two talking about? He's had girls falling all over him forever."

"I'm sure he has." Irene smiled, wise and calm. "Many would see his good looks. Some would appreciate his good heart. A few might sense he's much like his brother, Cahill."

"Exactly," Val said. "And he played the field with all of them. Until… until now."

Irene looked at her closely. "That worries you?"

"How could it? She's a lovely girl. Lovely. That's what everyone says. Her eyes especially."

"That's exactly what Eleanor said to me. That her eyes are an amazing color, like a flower blooming in your mother's garden…"

"Val?"

Only when Donna said her name did Val realize that Irene had let her comment about Kiernan's girlfriend's eyes trail off and now both women were watching her. Her thoughts had gone to another mention of flowers in her mother's garden. She hadn't made the connection—if there was one—before.

"Like delphinium. The ones in Mom's garden are amazing." She swallowed. "You call it larkspur out here."

The women exchanged a glance, then Donna put a hand on her arm. "It will be okay, Val."

Val rallied. "Of course it will. Everybody says she doesn't say much, but it's obvious from the way she looks at Kiernan that she's as crazy for him as he is for her. And there's no doubt he is head over heels for her. It will be a great match. A great match."

"It's your own match you should be thinking about," Donna said. "Not worrying about others, as much as you care about them."

Val felt a twinge of guilt. How could she explain that as much as she cared about Kiernan, words spoken by a woman she hardly knew had her spooked at another level.

I don't want to alarm you—you're such a nice couple—but I do see a connection to larkspur.

That had made it seem the woman meant them—her and Jack. Not Kiernan and his Felicity.

But that was crazy.

Completely and utterly crazy.

And she would not display a case of loopy Bridezilla nerves to these two solid, sane, staunch ranch women she so admired. She would not.

"Anyway, there's little you could do, my dear," Irene Weston said, with the calm of knowledge and experience. "As I said, Kiernan is like his brother. Like Cahill, when he finds the one, that is that."

WEDNESDAY

"C'mon, sleepyhead." Ethan flung back the curtains, letting glaring light pour into the room. "I've already been up, had a shower, and eaten breakfast."

Paige knew all that, because he'd asked her questions each step of the way—had she slept well, did she want to shower first, did she want him to wait for her to go to breakfast? It was his usual considerate way. But this time she'd uncharacteristically said no to each, adding that she didn't want any breakfast and she was going to catch some more sleep.

"Dave's ready to take us out on the horseback tour of the ranch you were so interested in last night at dinner."

Paige groaned and pulled a pillow over her face, returning to blessed dimness.

"Hurry up or you'll miss it. All the adults are going."

"Jack? Isn't he helping that horse," she mumbled. She didn't really care and it wouldn't change what she did. It was more that Ethan's cheerfulness unaccountably irritated her, he'd missed including the groom-to-be in "everybody," and she'd wanted to point that out to him.

"Right. Jack's going to catch up with us." His cheerfulness was unimpaired. "He's getting things ready for that abused horse that's being brought here. Seems like a strange wedding gift to me."

"No gifts. He likes to help abused horses," she muttered.

"I know. It was a joke."

"Ha. Ha."

"C'mon, Paige. You don't want to miss this. And you don't want to hold everybody up."

"Stop pushing me, Ethan. You're always pushing me."

"I am?"

He sounded so astonished it almost turned her mood. Almost.

And when it failed to do that, somehow it made everything worse.

"Yes, you are," she said shortly. Though he might not have heard that, since her voice was muffled by the pillow. "The only reason you don't recognize it is I usually go along. No resistance, so it doesn't feel like pushing to you. Just like normal—you getting your own way."

"You were all enthusiastic about this horseback tour last night."

"I changed my mind."

He'd come to her side of the bed and she knew he was looking down at her. "Only about riding this morning? Or more?"

"I don't know." She pushed off the pillow and sat up, her back to the window, not looking at Ethan.

"I thought you wanted to come to this wedding? If you didn't, you should have spoken up and I'd have held out, no matter what Hannah and Mandy said. We could still leave and—"

"No, we can't." She heard her own tone, sighed, then resumed in closer to her usual attitude, though with an overlay of weariness. "And I don't want to leave. They're wonderful people, it's terrific to see Dax and Hannah with their friends, and it's fun. I guess I'm still dragging from that food poisoning."

He sat beside her on the bed and put his arm around her. "That really hit you, didn't it? You usually bounce back fast. After the wedding, we'll get you in to Hannah and Dax's doctor."

"No, no that's not necessary. I don't feel anywhere as bad as I did when I had that bout. It's left me tired and my system's wonky."

"Want me to rub your shoulders?"

"My shoulders?"

"You told Hannah your shoulders were sore from the strap on your shoulder bag."

"That's not what—" She shook her head. "No, thanks. It's okay."

He kissed her forehead. "Want to take another nap?"

"As a matter of fact, I do. To go back to sleep, anyway."

He looked taken aback again for an instant. But he recovered quickly. "Okay. I'll go on this tour and leave you be to rest up more. Want the drapes closed?"

"Yes, please."

He kissed her again, this time lightly on the lips. On his way past the window, he pulled the drapes closed, returning the dimness.

"Thanks, Ethan." She sank back to the pillows.

He grinned at her from the door, though his eyes weren't entirely with the program. "Sure thing."

Planning the Wedding:

The Wedding Party's Outfits

Val walked in to the ranch office, saying a quick hello to Dave, who was checking for a title on the bookshelves behind his desk, and held out a swatch of material to Jack. "What color would you call this?"

Jack glanced at it. "The color of those dresses you picked for El and Matty to wear in the wedding."

The guy's outfits had been quickly agreed on: good jeans, polished boots, white shirts, matching vests, and cowboy hats.

In consultation with El and Matty, she'd decided on short dresses to be worn with cowboy boots. El had found a pair of boots nearly identical to Matty's at a boot store in Boston, which allowed her to break them in before the wedding. "But don't tell anyone here you bought them in Massachusetts," Val ordered.

For their dresses, she'd found one that offered varied necklines—a halter for El and a scoop with spaghetti straps for Matty—in the same color she loved.

It was that color she now held out to Jack.

"I know it's the color of their dresses. That's why I'm asking what you would call this color."

"Light green."

"Wrong answer," Dave said, without turning around.

"How can it be wrong? It's light green. Look."

Dave looked over Jack's shoulder at the swatch of fabric Valerie held. "Uh-huh. Very pretty. And it is a light green, but I'll guarantee it has a different name."

Val chuckled. "That's the issue. I don't know whether to tell the florist it's celadon or pine forest or seafoam or dusty sage or *eau ʋe nile* or even mint, though I don't think it's mint. But it could be new pine."

Jack looked taken aback. Dave said, "Take a picture and send it to the florist."

"Tried that. Don't know if it was her phone or my phone, but she said it came out blue. I put it on my blog—that's where all the names came for it—and then she said those are all different colors. I have to go in to Jefferson and show her."

"Okay, see you when you get back," Jack said, clearly thinking he was free to step away from the issue.

Dave laughed. When Jack looked around at him, he said, "I

think you'll find that your bride-to-be wants you to go with to discuss with the florist whether it's sage or pine or, uh, any of those other colors."

"Seafoam or celadon or—Okay, forget that for now. Would you mind coming with me? Of course I can go alone if you're too busy."

Jack looked at his boss.

Dave immediately raised his hands in surrender. "No way am I standing between a bride, wedding flowers, and the right color for dresses."

"One of them's for Matty," Val reminded him.

"Go. Take the rest of the day. Take my truck. Stay for dinner. On me. Just don't let my wife say I contributed in any way to a flower debacle."

Val chuckled. "Don't get too carried away. Matty's looking after Addie, so you'd have her for dinner, too."

"Fine with me. We love having her around."

"Oh, I know that. I'm not worried about you guys. It's *Jack* who'd be upset about missing her at dinner."

Dave joined her chuckle.

"Very funny, you two." Jack took off his hat and tapped Val's derriere with it. "Let's go see this lady about these flowers."

CHAPTER SEVEN

The horseback tour naturally divided into two groups.

Dave took the lead group, which included Kiernan, Dax, Ted Weston, neighboring rancher Cal Russkoff, Matty, and eventually Jack.

Ethan thought of them as the serious ranchers, with Kiernan included because he'd helped Jack with setting up computer apps to refine the tracking of the Slash-C/Flying W breeding programs. They were deep into discussion of that and the anticipated arrival of an abused horse that Jack would work with before they'd even left the corral area where mounts were selected or assigned.

Ethan thought of the other group—the one led by Ed and Donna, with Val, Hannah, Eleanor, Cahill, Irene, Mandy, neighbor and friend Taylor Larsen Russkoff, and a young couple named Zoe and Matt—as the tourists.

He was so far back at the end of that group that he might as well form a third group all by himself—the non-riders.

In fact, he discovered Matt was a former rodeo cowboy, for Pete's sake. Cahill had ridden as a kid, while Zoe, Hannah, Taylor, Irene, and Val knew what they were doing. Mandy, too, was holding her own. She hadn't been kidding about improving her riding skills with her visits to Wyoming.

If it hadn't been for the young ranch hand named Bryan—assigned the task of bringing up the rear and looking out for problems—Ethan would have been dead last.

He wished Paige were here.

She'd be wowed by this scenery, fascinated by how different it was from the Blue Ridge Mountains they knew.

She'd been looking forward to this, yet she'd chosen more sleep over coming. It was so unlike her.

Being sick was unlike her, too. And her slowness in bouncing back… Yeah, she was definitely seeing a doctor as soon as they could arrange it.

Either his horse had picked up speed, or Hannah was dropping back to come up next to him. He knew which of those options he'd bet on.

"How're you doing?" she asked. "You didn't get the best horse."

"Which showed good judgment—no way do I deserve a better horse. Buster and I are doing fine. Wish I could hear Ed and Donna better, but Bryan's filled in some for me, and this is a great way to see the country."

She smiled at him. "You are a good sport."

Surprised, he said a quick, "Thanks" then switched the subject. "Hannah, I'd like to get Paige in to your doctor when we get back to Bardville. Or—did I hear right that Zoe's the doctor in the nearest town?"

"Yes, she's gradually taking over the practice there. But—"

"Maybe that would be best. See if she could take a look at Paige today when we get back—"

"Wait a second. Did Paige say she wants to see a doctor? Now or in Bardville?"

"No, but this food poisoning must have been a lot worse than we thought. She's taking naps and she wanted to sleep in this morning."

Hannah laughed. "Ethan, you don't call the Mayo Clinic over naps, especially on vacation. Did you ask her about seeing a doctor?"

"Yeah. She said no, but this is unlike her—"

"So you're going to bulldoze over her and make her do what you've decided she should?"

He looked at her, startled. "Bulldoze? I'm trying to make sure she's okay. I want what's best for her."

She sighed. "It's like hearing myself talking about you and Mandy right after Mom and Dad died. I wanted to be *sure you were okay*. I wanted what *was best for you*. But I let your responses guide that, which meant I let it go too far."

"Let what go too far?"

As soon as he said it, he had a feeling he wasn't going to like her answer.

"Your taking over, that's what. You were lost and you needed the certainty, things you could count on. I let it go and let it go. And now it's a habit…"

He hitched a shoulder impatiently. "It's simply being organized and responsible."

"It's a crutch."

That didn't come from Hannah. Only when he heard Mandy's voice did he realize she'd also dropped back. Her horse was still some ahead of them, but close enough to hear.

"You use organization and responsibility as a crutch not to take any risks or—"

"Then it's one you should start using, because you're all over the place. No order, no schedule—"

"Schedule? Life is made up of the things not written in ink on your calendar, the things—"

"Ink? You're such a Luddite. It's all online. No ink involved."

"—that come in between those grid squares, that flow right over it, and erase everything else."

"Go away, Mandy," Hannah ordered. "Right now."

Mandy huffed, but she loosened her horse's reins and trotted up to join the main body of the tourists group.

"She's not all wrong," Hannah said quietly. "A plan's great, but it can't replace living. Organization and fiscal responsibility should serve your life and your emotions, not replace them. I understand, Ethan. Truly, I understand that you needed all that after the crash, but you took it too far. I'm responsible for letting you do that. And I regret it."

She'd startled him again. It was an odd experience hearing these Mandy-esque comments from her. "I'm a grown man, Hannah. You're not responsible—"

"I am. I let the habit become this deeply engrained in you. I suppose Paige, too, to an extent. We both saw that it helped you then. But I was the adult. I should have stopped it from taking you over."

"Nothing's taken me over. That's—"

"You're becoming inflexible, Ethan. And dictatorial. If Paige didn't love you so much, she'd hit you over the head with a skillet a dozen times a week. At least I know I would."

This went well past startled.

Before he could respond, though, Ed called to them to catch up to hear the story about how Lovesick Cowboy Creek got its name.

Hannah gave him a pointed look. "Loosen the reins, Ethan."

"I'm not holding him back."

"Not on the horse. Loosen the reins on yourself. And Paige."

Planning the Wedding:

The Flowers

In the little shop called Flower Power that sat across the street from the county courthouse in Jefferson, Val identified herself to the woman with graying hair.

"I remember you. Of course I do. Both of you." She beamed from her to Jack. "And now you're getting married and having a baby to add to your little girl."

"You remember her, too?" Val glanced at Jack as she asked that. He didn't look as surprised as she was.

"Indeed. How could I forget you? Such a charming family. Now, let's see this fabric."

A charming family. Wasn't that the phrase this woman had used last year when she and Addie and Jack had come into this shop? He'd been withdrawn, but only when he wasn't being cranky. Nobody seeing them then could have predicted that things would turn out the way they had.

Must be a phrase the flower shop woman used for everyone.

"The fabric?" she gently nudged.

Val pulled it out of her bag.

"Oh, yes, that's perfect."

The woman's delight was so genuine, Val smiled. "I agree. It looks great on both my bridesmaids. But nobody agrees on what to call it—cilantro, pale sage, seafoam, *eau ʋe nile,* pine forest... The list goes on and on."

"I would imagine that what each person calls it depends on her perspective—or his." The woman looked at Jack. "What do you call it?"

"Light green."

Val and the woman looked at each other and did a slight *men* eye-roll.

"I would expect that people from Wyoming might call it sage, though I would say pearled sage, rather than simply pale. Where—"

It was Jack's turn for a slight eye-roll. Val sucked the inside of her cheeks between her teeth to keep from chuckling. Thankfully, the woman had not seen his expression.

"—someone familiar with cooking might say cilantro and—"

"You're right. That's exactly what Mom and Manuela said first when they saw it."

"—those with other backgrounds or experiences would call it by other names."

"Yes, yes, yes. That's it exactly. El calls it seafoam. That's my cousin Eleanor—my matron of honor—and she lives by the ocean, in Massachusetts. But Matty always calls it sage, and she's from here. This all makes sense now."

Jack eyed the fabric. "Huh. I can sort of see that. The way the waves look in some lights. And I guess it is a little like faded sage."

"Pearled sage," the two women said in unison.

"It will look lovely with your flowers," added the woman from the shop.

"But I haven't picked any flowers yet."

The woman didn't seem to hear her. "I've been nurturing something special for your wedding flowers."

Val blinked. "You have? But I only called last week…"

"Yes, dear. Come this way. Both of you."

Val glanced at Jack. He shrugged and gestured for her to go ahead of him.

The woman led them through the back to outside, where a garden occupied the space between the shop and the back of the house behind it, which faced the opposite street. Close to the shop were raised beds, packed with plants.

The woman led them along a narrow path to a shed that formed the left-hand edge of the garden. Opening its door, she said, "Come in, come in. I don't want too much of the warm air to get in."

They stepped down several steps and the temperature dropped as they went. The shed, Val realized, was built down and into the side of a small hill, providing natural cooling.

"What have you considered for flowers?" The woman asked the question, but Val had the odd feeling that her answer wasn't going to matter a lot.

"I haven't thought specifically. The wedding's going to be outside—we hope. Or if the weather's bad, in the Slash-C barn. Something simple." Impulsively, she added, "And something cheerful."

"Naturally. A base of white daisies, which promise cheerfulness." She stared at Jack, then Val before saying, "And mums, which stand for loyalty. Oh, yes, and you must have everlasting love represented by baby's breath. And at least a few white roses. They *are* the bridal rose, after all. Those will also make up the attendant's bouquets. But for yours..." She reached back into a dim corner behind other pots and brought one out. "...we will add this."

There were no blooms at all. It was simply a green plant. Though it did seem familiar. "Is that..? Is that a monkeyflower plant?"

"It is, indeed." The woman beamed at her.

"We came in here to get monkeyflower for Matty, remember Jack?"

He glanced toward the woman, then cleared his throat, before he answered her. "For Matty and then I got more for in front of the cottage. For you. I remember."

They smiled at each other, then Val turned back to the woman. "But how on earth did you remember?"

"How could I not? *Mimulus guttatus.* Yellow common monkeyflower."

"Good for turning someone who's too cautious into someone who lives with cheerful enthusiasm. I certainly remember *that*," Val said. *Cheerful.* Huh. Strange that's what she'd said she wanted the bouquet to be. "But they'll be past their main blooming time by August won't they? Judging by last year, there might a few blooms, the way you said, but mostly past by the wedding."

"That's why I've kept these pots—" She gestured to the dimness, which might have been occupied by a brigade of pots for all Val could tell. "—in here. All prepared to bloom when I give them more light, just before your wedding."

Tears came into Val's eyes. "That's so kind of you. I don't know how you could have known, but I can't think of any flower I'd want more in my bridal bouquet."

The woman beamed again, then turned brisk. "They'll be ready right on time, but for now, they've had enough excitement." She replaced the pot, then gestured with one hand toward the door. "Come, come, back to the shop."

"Addie will love the monkeyflowers," Jack said as the single-file path widened near the back door.

"Over the moon," Val agreed. "And they'll look lovely with the white flowers you mentioned, though perhaps something darker for contrast or—"

"Oh dear."

The woman had stopped. She seemed to be looking at Jack and her. Or through them. Her gaze was unfocused, yet intense.

"Oh, dear. Oh, dear. Oh, dear."

As Val started to turn to see what Jack was making of this, the woman blinked and said, "Inside. Come inside."

She waved a hand to hurry them, then gestured for them

to go to the other side of the counter, while she went behind it, turning her back to them. She reached up to run her finger over the spines of books housed on shelves. "I don't want to alarm you—you're such a nice couple—but I do see a connection to larkspur."

"Larkspur? That's not a flower I'm familiar with. Are you saying for the contrast color—"

"There." The woman placed an open book before her.

The color was an intense blue with an extra touch of lavender that made you want to dive into it and lose yourself.

"Oh, I know that flower. That's delphinium. I haven't seen it around here, but my mom plants delphinium in her garden in Gloucester. She's so proud that they bloom like crazy for her. But I don't think—"

"She plants them? On purpose?" Jack sounded disapproving.

"Delphinium is the genus, larkspur is the common name, and there are many, many varieties. Here in Wyoming, though, it is largely not welcomed." The woman looked at Jack.

Val turned to do the same. He nodded. "Poisonous to cattle. Real poisonous."

Val looked back at the picture. "It is? Well, not a lot of cattle roaming Gloucester, so that's not a problem. Unless there *use* to be lots of cattle and the delphiniums or—What did you call it?"

"Larkspur. You don't see it around here because we work real hard to keep it out. Especially since cattle love it. Not good for horses, either. But they won't go to town eating it the way cattle do. Still, if they get some it can be bad, especially if they start running after eating it. Got to keep them real calm and quiet to try to let it work out of their systems."

"Indeed, it is poisonous also for dogs and cats. Humans, as well," the woman finished in a clear afterthought.

Val met Jack's eyes, then had to look away fast to avoid laughing. She cleared her throat. "What part's poisonous?"

"All of it—seeds, flower, leaves. Seeds and the first growth are the worst. Toxic cocktail of alkaloids." Jack didn't sound like laughing anymore.

"Wow. Why didn't I ever hear about this? Since it's poisonous to people, you'd think I'd have heard that. Like foxglove or lily of the valley."

"People don't eat it like cattle do," Jack said.

"That's quite true. Why, even the Native Americans, who found many uses for every plant they encountered, would not take it internally, though they did grind it up and use it topically to kill lice. In addition, it is associated with fickleness, so perhaps they stayed away from it for that reason."

"Oh-kay." Val drew it out. "Kills cattle and lice, stands for fickle. Larkspur *and* delphinium are definitely out of the bouquets. But I do want some stronger color against the yellow and white."

"Ah, yes, I can see that you would." The woman leaned back and looked from one to the other of them. "What I would recommend is the flower that stands for love and devotion, which will also give you color to set off the yellow and white.

Red roses."

Into a comfortable silence on the way back to the Slash-C, Val said, "Strange to think something as pretty as those larkspur flowers could hurt something as big as a cow."

"Not just hurt. Kill. No known treatment to cure them. You have to let it run its course and most times it ends up with the animal dead. Some ranchers have taken heavy losses that way if they're not careful about their rangeland."

"I wonder if I should tell Mom about her delphiniums being poisonous."

"Just be sure she doesn't add any to salads or start chewing on seeds."

"You're right. Why ruin her pleasure in something beautiful when it's unlikely to ever cause a problem for her."

As she drifted off to sleep, she had the thought that the Flower Power woman had never explained what she'd meant about seeing larkspur associated with them.

She didn't think about it again until her conversation with Donna and Irene about eyes the color of flowers in her mother's garden.

CHAPTER EIGHT

Paige had gotten herself up and dressed before the riders returned with lots of enthusiastic accounts of the sights they'd seen.

She felt a twinge at missing the ride.

Offsetting that was not being able to even imagine having the energy to have gotten on a horse this morning.

Now feeling somewhat better, she, Matty, Val, Taylor, Mandy, and Hannah were crossing from the main house, where they'd cleaned up after a huge lunch for all the guests as well as the ranch hands, to the barn to get quilts being temporarily stored there and hang them out to air.

"We'd hoped to air them outside in the open, but with those clouds piling up, we're going to play it safe and air them on Matty and Dave's porch," Val said.

"What are the quilts for?" Hannah asked.

"They'll cushion the hay bales we're using for seating at the ceremony and for extra seating around during the reception. And then…" Matty let it trail off as she watched a large truck rumble up the drive.

They all stopped and stared at it.

"What on earth is that?" Val pointed to what the truck was towing. It resembled a large motorhome, but with only small windows set high up on one side and—they saw when the truck followed the drive's curve and they saw the other side—multiple sets of doors on the other.

Matty chuckled. "That's Ed's surprise for you and Jack. Let him explain. Brennan," she called to her older son. "Go get Grandpa and tell him his surprise has arrived."

The boy dashed to the building Paige now knew was the office and in a second, not only Ed Currick, but Dave Currick and Jack Ralston, followed by Dax, Ted, and her Ethan came out.

At the same time, Donna and Irene came out of Donna's house.

"It's here," Ed said, with the enthusiasm of a boy at Christmas.

"*What* is here?" Val asked.

"Just a minute, just a minute. Let me talk to the driver first."

While he did that—with all the men accompanying him—Val tried to pry out of Donna and Matty what it was. They wouldn't divulge Ed's secret.

Finally, after consultations that appeared serious and thorough, Ed clapped Dave on the back, apparently deputizing him to carry out the instructions. The other men stayed with the truck, but Ed drew Jack with him as he returned to the knot of women.

"I can't take it another second, Ed," Val said. "What is that thing?"

"That, my dear Valerie, is our gift—"

"Don't include me in this," Donna said.

"No gifts," Val objected.

"All right, all right. Make it *my contribution* to the celebration of you and Jack getting married."

Matty, appearing to fight laughter said, "But you haven't told them yet what it is, Ed."

"Oh, right. It's a top of the line four-stall portable restroom. Flush toilets, running water, self-contained plumbing so no strain on the septic system, air-conditioning and heat if we need it, outdoor lighting, they even have hand soaps and towels."

The last items were too much for his wife and daughter-in-law. Who started laughing first was unclear, but they fed off each other.

"It's a porta potty on steroids," Matty giggled.

"The man has been obsessed about ordering the right one. He canceled one because he didn't like the lighting."

Jack cleared his throat. "Seems practical. What with all the guests and such who'll be here over the weekend."

"Practical?" Val repeated. "*Practical?* It's brilliant. Absolutely and completely *brilliant.*"

She threw her arms around Ed's neck and kissed him on the cheek.

He reddened with delight, tossing a triumphant look at his wife, who laughingly conceded his victory.

"You all go ahead and start on the quilts," Val added. "I want to see every feature of this mobile restroom—especially the lighting and the hand soaps and guest towels. C'mon, Ed, give me the grand tour."

Planning the Wedding:
The Rings

Jack lifted her hand from where it rested on his chest in the aftermath of making love.

"You need a ring."

"I'll get one at the wedding," she said sleepily.

"Yeah, I need to get you one for that, too. But you should have an engagement ring."

She lifted her head and kissed his chin, which was as far as she could reach. "If we use the money we have saved for the wedding on a ring we'll have to push back the wedding.

"We've saved some other money—"

"That's not for wedding stuff. That's for college for the kids."

"—and I have that account—"

"That's for emergencies."

He sighed. "You need a ring."

"Not until the wedding, I don't. Then we'll get plain bands and we'll be all set."

She was almost asleep, having settled the matter in her own mind, when he said softly, "I have an idea."

"Mmm." She burrowed against him. "Okay."

Valerie Trimarco had not lied about her family.

Neither had Donna Currick.

Unloading from the various trucks that had gone to pick them up at the airport, they descended on the Slash-C *en masse*, with laughter, love, teasing, and strong Boston accents.

Gloucester accents, as one immediately corrected Paige.

Lucy Trimarco, a dynamo even shorter than her daughter, engulfed Eleanor, Cahill, and Kiernan in hugs.

"For Pete's sake, Mom, you saw them earlier this week in Gloucester," Val protested.

"I'm glad to see them *now*."

"She hugs us like this whenever she sees us at home," Eleanor said.

"Whose side are you on?" Val asked.

"Both," Eleanor said immediately.

Lucy reached up and patted her cheek, while Jimmy Trimarco murmured, "Always was a smart girl, our Eleanor."

"And Felicity? Where is she?" Lucy demanded of Kiernan.

"She's coming in tomorrow."

"She didn't come with you? Why not? You're not letting that one slip away are you? Or are you following your usual ways of—No, no, I see you're still as crazy about her as ever. Just see that you stay that way and don't lose her."

"Yes, Aunt Lucy." Kiernan's docility had a glint of deviltry in it.

"Always was a smart boy," Jimmy murmured again.

Cahill was hiding a grin as he said, "Let's get you all over to the Flying W and get you settled."

"You haven't been there yet?" Hannah asked.

"Mom insisted on coming here right away to see where the wedding's going to be first," Val said with fatalism.

"And it's gorgeous," Lucy said. "Those mountains! And look at all this sky. It's like being on the ocean but with the ground under your feet. I feel much better about my baby getting married so far from home."

"Mom, this is home, too." Val softened the words with a hand on her mother's shoulder.

"Would've had to come by here first even if Mom wasn't being all emotional," Val's brother Anthony said. "We needed to drop off dinner."

Val spun around to him, appearing torn between suspicion and amusement. "What are you talking about?"

"Talking about surf and turf."

"I know about the turf, but you're a long way from surf in case you didn't notice that while you traveled west all day."

"I noticed. That's why I checked them."

"You checked—? What did you check?"

"Lobsters."

"*Lobsters?*"

"Yup. For dinner."

"Your crazy brother slipped minimal clothes into my suitcase, then used his suitcase limit to bring a crate of lobster," explained her long-suffering sister-in-law.

"Yeah, and they won't last 'til tomorrow, so everybody's gotta eat up tonight."

"You sprung this on Matty and—?"

"Heck, no. Matty and I worked it all out weeks and weeks ago."

"Surprise," Matty said with a grin. "Consider this one of your surprise reception surprises, Val."

The others had gone to the Flying W to drop off their bags before dinner, but Lucy Trimarco opted to stay at the Slash-C home ranch for a tour of Jack and Valerie's new house, given by Val and Eleanor.

At the end, she said, "When you said logs, I worried, but it's very nice."

"Logs doesn't mean a dirt floor these days, Mom."

"*Dirt* floor? I should hope not. How would you ever keep it clean?"

Val opened her mouth, then thought better of it. Behind Lucy's back, Eleanor gave her a nod of approval. Val rolled her eyes in response.

And was almost caught at it as her mother turned to her abruptly.

"How are you, dear? How are you *really*?" her mom asked, studying her face.

"I'm fine, Momma. Happy, healthy, and looking forward to being married to Jack."

Lucy hugged her again. "I can see the truth of all that. And the baby? Without a doctor out here—"

"Oh, I have a doctor." She touched her belly. "We have a doctor. You'll meet her this weekend. She's great."

"A woman doctor? Way out here?"

"Absolutely. Zoe Parisi. She's terrific."

"I met her this morning, Aunt Lucy," Eleanor added, holding open the door to the front porch for the others. "She's a brilliant young doctor."

"How young?" the older woman demanded.

"Very young," Eleanor said calmly. "What's more important is how brilliant. And she's very brilliant. Dedicated, too. And she's involved in a terrific new remote medical program that gives them access to the top medical facilities and minds in the country."

Lucy dismissed the program with a *humph* that said she expected no less for her daughter and not-yet-born grandchild.

Before she could express that, however, El diverted the older woman's attention.

"I'm glad you're here, Aunt Lucy, because now Valerie will stop pestering me with questions about Kiernan's Felicity."

Val admired her cousin's approach to dealing with Lucy Trimarco. It was a heck of a lot more effective than her head-to-head straight-on confrontation tactic. She wished she'd remember that before she went head-to-head with her mother.

"Oh, Felicity." Lucy turned to Val. "Isn't she wonderful?"

"I haven't met her, remember? But, since you've had a chance to get to know her all spring and summer, Mom, what do you think?"

Her mother glanced toward El, then away. "Like I said, she's wonderful. You look at the two of them together and they're the perfect couple. Like a magazine or a movie. Clear as day that Kiernan's mad for her. But there's nothing conceited about her. You can talk to her just like anyone else."

Val doubted there was anyone her mother couldn't talk to. A gene she'd inherited, she recognized ruefully. And it seemed Addie had as well.

"Maybe a touch reserved," Lucy continued, "though she has such lovely manners. And there's no denying she's a gorgeous thing, what with those Elizabeth Taylor eyes. Though more blue, I'd say, than true violet. They look exactly like my delphiniums. Oh, Donna's waving me over to the big house. Shall we all go?"

"It's probably about cooking the lobsters. You go on ahead, Mom. We'll be there soon."

Eleanor touched her arm. "What's bothering you, Val?"

"Partly what's bothering me is that you're not saying what's worrying you about Kiernan. Kiernan and presumably this girlfriend, Felicity."

"Nothing's worrying me—"

"Hah. Okay, I get it. You don't want to talk about it."

"There's nothing to talk about. If I had something that could be put in words... Besides—" Her tone switched. "—there was something else that bothered you. You jumped about six inches while Aunt Lucy was telling you about Felicity. Are you sure—?"

"All your imagination."

Eleanor didn't buy it. "Not my imagination. You jumped when she was talking about Felicity's eyes."

Delphinium. Larkspur.

Oh dear. Oh dear. Oh dear.

She'd heard the concern in the flower shop woman's voice. Seen it in her eyes.

I don't want to alarm you—you're such a nice couple—but I do see a connection to larkspur.

Had the woman have picked up something to do with Kiernan and this woman who seemed to have won his heart?

Good grief. What was she thinking? No wonder she hadn't told El. It sounded far-fetched in her own head, much less spoken aloud.

She needed to keep her focus on having her friends and family here. Which, judging from the tenor of her mother's call to Eleanor and her, meant helping Wyomingites cook and eat Massachusetts lobsters.

Dinner was under cover as a rainstorm parked over them while most of the visible sky remained clear.

The lobster was a hit with all the adults.

Some of the kids shied away from it. Though, after watching Addie and two of her cousins eat it with gusto, Brennan Currick tried it and liked it, too.

"That was a mistake," Dave said morosely.

"What?"

"Letting my kid get a taste for lobster."

That feast was topped with a universal winner—ice cream cones, with Ed and Dave digging the scoops out of five gallon buckets.

Now that the rain had passed. The porch steps were packed like bleacher seats, with more occupying chairs, rockers, and benches on the half of the porch not occupied by quilts.

All to watch the spectacle of the setting sun turning clouds ever changing colors.

"Sunset seems later here, even with the sun dropping behind the mountains," Val's dad said.

"It is. Nearly half an hour this time of year. Sunrise is a bit earlier, too," Jack said. "Longer days here spring and summer, closer to the same in winter."

Silence settled as they consumed their cones and watched the sky.

"What's that light?" Anthony asked from his seat on the porch steps with his second cone. He was looking considerably lower than the clouds.

"You mean you don't recognize it?" Val demanded.

Stepping in to forestall a sibling dispute, Taylor Larsen Ruskoff said, "Those are lightning bugs."

"Fireflies," chorused several of the Wyoming natives.

"Whatever you call them," Anthony said, "I didn't think you had them out here."

"You folks east of the Mississippi do keep most of them to yourselves," Ed said.

That caused a spurt of chuckles.

"Heck," he continued, "according to some scientists, they're not here at all. But they must not have looked too closely. We have a couple warm springs back behind the barn that help them get through the winter. Still, it's harder on them here. That's why they're flashing so slowly."

"And if you'd been here in June," Dave added, "you would hardly see them at all, because when they start flashing it's still light and you can't see them."

"That's gotta be tough on a guy bug trying to attract a girl bug around here," Val's brother, Bobby, said.

"Oh, we do okay." Dave put his arm around Matty and squeezed as the others laughed.

CHAPTER NINE

With the promise of a long day on Thursday, a caravan of trucks left, taking those staying at the Flying W on the short trip. Those staying on the Slash-C first bundled the quilts onto Matty's kitchen table in case of overnight rain, then began to head to the individual houses where they were staying.

"Have a minute, Paige?" Hannah asked.

"Of course."

Ethan turned around when the two of them stopped. "What's up?"

"Really, Ethan," Hannah scolded mildly.

"All right, all right. I'll leave a light in the window."

They all chuckled as he headed off alone.

Hannah took her by the arm and led her away over to the edge of where an overhead light stretched its illumination to part of a corral fence enclosing a couple of placid looking horses.

When Paige shifted focus from the horses to Ethan's older sister, she was hit instantly by that strange look again.

The same one Hannah had given her during that discussion about her shoulder bag's strap.

Paige hadn't given that look much thought in the past two days. When she hadn't been busy, she'd been asleep.

But now that the look had cropped up again, she considered it.

Puzzled.

At least it held an element of puzzlement, Paige decided.

And *speculative?* Yeah, she thought that, too.

But also with elements of concern and … excitement?

Add them together and you got … *strange.*

"Is something wrong, Hannah?" she asked.

"That's what I want to ask you—is something wrong?"

"Huh? You've lost me."

"You've seemed … different."

Paige shook her head. "I don't know why I would. Nothing's changed."

"Hmm." Hannah's sound held skepticism, but not enough to argue with. "Your shoulder bag—"

Paige's sound mixed amusement and disbelief. "Back to that? It's the usual—"

"Yes, back to that," Hannah interrupted. "The bag being heavy has never bothered you before. And if that was the reason it was causing you discomfort, it would have been your shoulder that hurt, right?"

"Sure, but what—?"

"Where has it been hurting?"

"I haven't even been aware there *was* any discomfort until you brought it up."

"Do you know what you'd been doing that caught Donna's attention?" After Paige's head shake, Hannah answered her own question. "You kept running your hand down the strap, pulling it away from you." She demonstrated the move with an imaginary strap.

"Did I? I don't know why—Oh, wait. I bet you're right. I've been a little sore. My breasts. You know how you get sometimes during the month."

Hannah's *uh-huh* was devoid of a single drop of agreement.

At a loss, Paige just looked at her.

"Paige, I've known you since you were a child. I know you nearly as well as I know Mandy. The times your breasts have been tender before, it's always the same time, right? And this isn't that time, right?"

She double-checked her mental calendar. "No."

"Some women get early signals, long before tests can show anything, and that's one of the signals.

"Signals?" For an instant, Paige didn't get it.

Then she did.

She laughed.

An honest laugh, even though somewhere way down deep she felt the powerful ache.

She pushed it aside with facts. With reason. With reality.

"Oh, Hannah. No. You know what the doctors said. They left no doubt that getting pregnant was going to be a problem for us because of my issues. That's why Ethan's factored in treatments to try for two children in our financial projections."

Hannah didn't join her laughter.

Her small, wise smile gave Paige pause.

"Besides," Paige added, "I'm off kilter because of that food poisoning.

"*Was* it food poisoning?"

"Of course it was. Or a twenty-four-hour bug." She felt something rising up in her that she pushed down hard and firm. "There's no other explanation. The doctors didn't mince words."

"Did they say absolutely that you could not get pregnant without treatments?"

"They said almost surely."

Only after Hannah lifted a brow did Paige realize she could have ended this if she'd said, "Yes, they did."

"Almost surely," Hannah said quietly, "is not the same as absolutely. And sometimes nature has a way of turning even absolutely on its head. Think about it. Think about how you've felt this past week or so. You haven't been like your normal self and there have been signs— No, I'm not going to say more. I don't want to push my thoughts on you, Paige, but I want you to think about it."

Planning the Wedding:

The Guest List

"You just invite whoever you want," Jack said.

"No way. I have a list. And you have a list."

"I don't have—"

"Yes, you do. You sit down and write a list of who you want to be at our wedding. Don't go getting all practical on me about how they can't take time away from their ranch or any-thing. Write down the names and I'll take care of the rest."

"I will. Tonight."

"Now."

"Val—Fine. This shouldn't take long."

It took longer than he expected. And it included more names than he'd ever expected. But there it was. A list of names, along with a few addresses that he placed in front of her as she sat at the cleared kitchen table, folding clothes.

She looked at it for a beat, then jumped up from her chair, threw her arms around his neck, and kissed him.

When they both came up for air, he said, "I could go write another list if you want."

She laughed. "I'm so happy that you know you're connected to people. I love you, Jack Ralston."

Neither of them got any work done for quite a while.

Paige approached the issue the way she had approached most issues since Ethan had become a factor—*the* factor—in her life.

She would make a list.

Not immediately, though, because Ethan was still awake when she came out of the bathroom after getting ready for bed.

"Everything okay?" he asked.

"Yes." Then she answered his real question. "You have to ask Hannah, but if she wanted you to know she would have already told you."

"Don't I know it."

She smiled at him, then picked up her device, turned on the light beside the easy chair, and sat. "I'm going to read for a while."

A flash of hurt crossed his face that surprised her, then it was gone. "Probably been getting so much sleep lately, now you can't fall asleep."

"That's probably it," she agreed.

"Your schedule's going to be all messed up when we get home."

"It is."

He looked at her for a moment longer. "Good night, Paige. I love you."

"I love you, too. Sleep well."

He grunted an acknowledgement of her wish, switched off the bedside lamp, and pulled the sheet up over his shoulder.

As usual, he fell asleep almost immediately.

Paige put aside the device and pulled out a pad and pen. There was nothing like paper for list-making.

Hannah wanted her to think about how she'd been feeling this past week? Fine. She would.

First, she wrote food poisoning.

She considered that. It was a conclusion. To make the list rational and beneficial, she should probably focus on symptoms.

She crossed out *food poisoning* and wrote *nauseated* and *intestinal cramping.*

Was that totally accurate?

Her pen hesitated, then she added a question mark after *nauseated.*

Though that wasn't where her real doubt centered.

After a long moment, she crossed out *intestinal,* leaving cramping on its own.

Come to think of it, that wasn't the first odd thing. The morning before they'd left to come here, Ethan had opened his suitcase on the bed to start packing and the scent of the sachets she put in their suitcases to prevent mustiness had nearly knocked her over.

He'd laughed when she'd aired hers out for hours before packing, saying the scent was the same it always was.

It hadn't been. It had been much stronger. And it had made her queasy.

Or had that been hunger?

Could have been hunger. Must have been hunger.

Though that didn't explain the super nose.

She wrote *sachet scent* above the previous first item.

She added *sore breasts*. On the other hand, that wasn't unheard of by any means. Though, as Hannah had pointed out, this wasn't the right time.

She drew an arrow to an open space and wrote *weird timing*.

Then she stopped.

See that wasn't much.

Okay, there'd been that moment the first morning in Wyoming when they took an early walk with Sarah and she'd cried because the birdsong was so beautiful. But surely that wasn't worth adding…

Ethan had hinted she was cranky. That had been when she … Oh, yeah, when she took a nap the other afternoon.

Actually, she wouldn't mind a nap right now. Close her eyes for a moment and…

She jerked awake at the sound of rain on the roof, with the pad still in her hand, but the pen AWOL.

After hunting around, she found it on the floor.

She read the short list. Argued with herself.

Finally added *emotional, cranky*, and *naps*. She decided not to add sleeping in. She figured *naps* covered it.

The list was messy.

It also looked more substantial than she would have liked.

Time to check the Internet.

But not tonight. If Ethan woke up and asked what she was looking at…

Besides, she couldn't keep her eyes open any longer. She stashed away the list, turned out the light, and slipped into bed.

Ethan turned to her in his sleep, and they curled together.

CHAPTER TEN

THURSDAY

"Lots to do today," Matty reminded them at breakfast. "We need all the prep finished before the kids' rodeo this afternoon."

"Our kids don't know rodeo," protested Val's brother, Bobby.

"They'll catch on. And they'll love it." She grinned, and her sisters-in-law relaxed immediately.

"A rodeo? With kids? Isn't that dangerous?" Val's mother looked dubious.

"Wait until you see it. And tonight we'll have line dancing lessons so everyone will feel comfortable dancing Saturday night."

"It would take a lot more than one night to make me comfortable," Ethan said.

Val nudged him, with a grin. "You'll want to dance at your wedding, so you might as well start learning tonight."

"My wedding's years off. Plenty of time to step on Paige's toes before that."

"Don't be such a killjoy," Mandy said.

Simultaneously, Paige said, "Don't be such a grouch."

From Ethan's startled look, Val suspected Mandy's comment was no surprise, but Paige's was.

"Okay," he said slowly, "I won't be a grouch—"

"Or a killjoy," Mandy slipped in.

"—and I'll start learning to dance tonight."

"Great," Val said. "First thing is for everybody to help get the quilts hung back up on the porch."

That left the table clear for planned cooking and baking sessions inside, while lights were strung and more setup happened outside.

A few hours into the labor, Taylor stopped abruptly beside the table where the choppers were chopping for the massive amounts of potato salad planned.

"Val? What's wrong?" asked Taylor, who was responsible for carrying the chopped items back to the mixers and keeping the choppers resupplied with foods needing chopping.

"Onions," Anthony's wife said wisely from her seat down the table chopping celery.

"It's not the onions," Val said.

"You always cry when you chop onions."

"Okay, yes, it *is* the onions, partly. But even more than that, it's all of you being here. You and Tanya," she said to her sisters-in-law, "and Mom and Taylor and Zoe and El and Hannah and Mandy and Paige and Donna and Irene. And everybody. Ruth, who's not here because she's riding herd on the kids and—"

"Herd is right," muttered Matty.

"—the guys all out there working hard. And all our neighbors who've brought quilts and tables and dishes and more than I can even think of. All for Jack and me." She sniffled loudly.

Hannah handed her a box of tissues.

Lucy bustled over to her, put an arm around her shoulders and said, "You'll feel better when we start on the brownies and you can have some chocolate."

"Chocolate?" Val repeated longingly.

Everyone laughed at that, including Val, though tears still stood in her eyes.

The back door opened, held by Jack to let two newcomers in.

"Look who's here," he announced.

"Lisa! Shane!" several voices called.

Donna and Ed's daughter beamed around the room, but went straight to Val, who'd risen. They hugged warmly.

"Lisa has something—" Jack started from behind her, then got a better look at Val's face. "You've been crying. What's wrong?"

"Nothing. Nothing's wrong. It's onions."

"And pregnancy hormones," Anthony's wife added.

"And happiness," Lucy concluded, reaching up to pat his shoulder.

"Are you sure? Val? Are you okay?"

"I'm fine. Thrilled to see Lisa and Shane. More hands to chop," she teased.

"Uh, I think I'm needed outside," Shane said with a twinkle in his eyes. But he didn't make any move to leave.

In fact, he nudged Jack in the side.

"Oh, right," Jack said. "Uh, Lisa has something for you, Val."

Lisa shook her head, even as she took a small, beautifully wrapped box out of her bag and handed it to Val. "I'm just the conduit. It's from Jack."

Val looked up at him, but his eyes were on the box. He cleared his throat. "Open it."

Her fingers trembled, but she got the bow and ribbon off, slid away the paper, then tipped up the hinged cover.

She gasped.

Three rings were inside, two wedding bands and a diamond. The yellow diamond was on a slender white gold band that nestled with the smaller wedding band, so both bands showed white gold edges with gold between.

"There's a design…" Someone said from over her shoulder. "On both bands."

She looked at it closer.

Her head came up, she looked from Jack to Lisa and back. "Yellow monkeyflower. Oh, my God. An original design by Lisa Currick. Oh, Jack. What have you done?"

She burst into tears.

Jack looked horrified. "I should have waited until we were alone. I should have had you design your own. I should have—"

"Stop. Stop, Jack. That's not why I'm crying. They're beautiful. Gorgeous. Beyond perfect."

"Then why—?"

"Because you're beautiful. You're gorgeous. You're—"

She threw herself at him and he caught her, her words muffled by her mouth being against his shirt.

"Was that last one *beyond perfect?*" he asked.

"No, it was *an idiot.* And I love you."

"Jack, to ask Lisa, to—"

"All I did was call and—"

Donna had guided Val and Jack out to the porch. Lisa and Shane followed.

Val said, "You shouldn't have asked—"

"All he asked me was if I could help him find rings," Lisa said. "That's when I told him I would never forgive him if he didn't let me make your rings."

"But, Lisa, you can't—"

"It's our gift to you both."

"No gifts," Val said promptly.

"Val." Jack's single word was a remonstration.

"But—"

"She wanted to do this," Shane said quietly.

Tears came back into Val's eyes. "How can we ever thank—"

"You can wear them in happiness," Lisa said firmly.

Val hesitated a moment, then hugged the other woman.

"It's about time you finished objecting," Donna said from the doorway. "The woman with the flowers called and said she's almost here."

CHAPTER ELEVEN

When Paige finished her chopping quota before anyone else, Matty had asked her to help unload the Flower Power delivery van into a borrowed refrigerator in the barn.

She'd hesitated for a fraction of a second, as if she'd had something else she wanted to do, but before Val could give her an out from that task, she agreed to it with a smile.

Val, too, finally escaped the kitchen—and onions—and spotted Paige and the Flower Power woman returning from the barn. At one of the corrals, several of the men were preparing for today's kid's rodeo. Jack and Dax were visible at the distant corral they were preparing for the arrival this afternoon of his latest rescue project.

"I was just coming to look at the flowers. I can't wait," she called out to the two women.

Paige held up a stop-sign hand keeping her on the porch. "Matty said you're absolutely not allowed to peek."

"But they're my flowers. I ordered them and—"

"Not all of them," the woman from the flower shop said firmly. "You'll see them all on Saturday."

"But—"

Donna came out of the kitchen from behind her. "No buts. Matty sent me out to be sure you're not looking at the flowers. Also," she added with a smile to Paige, "because Hannah asked to see if you could help her with folding the napkins when you finished with the flowers. She said you know a special way."

Again Val had a sense of a momentary hesitation from Paige, then she returned Donna's smile, said, "Of course," and jogged up the steps and inside.

From behind Val, Donna said to the flower woman, "I'm sorry, I never even got your name."

"Myrtha Larchmont."

"I'm Donna Currick. And I want to thank you, Myrtha." Val turned at the deepened note of emotion in Donna's voice. "Thank you for everything."

"It's the flowers, ma'am. They're the powerful ones."

"Donna, what—?"

Too late. Donna had already given her a quick smile and gone back inside.

"Myrtha? What—"

"You wouldn't see much looking at your flowers now, anyway," the Flower Power woman said, returning to that topic. "They're still tightly closed up. There's a schedule of when to open which packages, so they'll be in full bloom at the right time. The bouquets are toward the back, so they'd be hard to get to, anyway. I do, however, have photos for you. If you'd like to see them."

She held out her phone.

If she'd like to see them?

Oh, yeah, she knew it was to distract her from asking questions. Didn't matter. She was down the steps in record time.

"This is what the real bouquet looked like right before I closed it up, but *this* is the trial run I made to test the timing and what it should look like Saturday."

"Ohhhhh." The real bouquet had been disappointing, appearing mostly green with many gaps, but this—this was "Gorgeous. Thank you so much. The yellow monkeyflowers are perfect."

"They all will be, come Saturday," the woman said with certainty. Then she looked directly at Val. "Have you seen any larkspur?"

"No. Of course not. You know how they work to keep it off the grazing land."

Myrtha's eyes narrowed. "But something's reminding you of larkspur."

"Sort of. Maybe. I don't know."

The woman patted her arm. "Larkspur trouble is coming for sure, but you're strong enough. You and him and monkeyflower. You'll do."

"Thank you." She smiled, yet still felt oddly weepy. Or maybe not so oddly considering her hormones. Impulsively, she added, "If there's ever anything I can do for you…?"

The woman tipped her head. "I was wondering… The young woman who helped me bring the flowers in…?"

"Paige. She and her fiancé are guests for the wedding."

"Have you known them long?"

"Not long. But I like her a lot. She's engaged to the groomsman's brother-in-law. They're a lovely couple, willing to help, and very nice." Val smiled. "Also very much in love."

"Oh, yes, yes." Myrtha Larchmont said, as if she'd already known that. "Would you mind if I had a word with her young man."

"Mind? Me? Of course not. Though I'm not sure exactly where—"

At that moment, Ethan walked around the corner of the barn.

"Ethan," Val called out immediately. She shot a look at the woman in the Flower Power shirt. She did not look surprised at this opportune appearance.

"Need help?" he asked cheerfully as he neared the porch.

"I do, young man," Myrtha said immediately.

"Yes, ma'am. Ms….?"

"This is Myrtha Larchmont. She did the flowers for the wedding. And this is Ethan Chalmers."

"Right this way, young man." The woman gestured him toward the van, then turned back to Val. "Remember, you're strong enough. You'll have a wonderful day on Saturday. And the days beyond that."

Val felt more tears come to her eyes, but she smiled as she hugged the woman. "Thank you for everything."

She should have gone inside then.

It was clear Myrtha had something to say to Ethan. But he *was* her wedding guest and if there was something odd…

Oh, heck, she just had to know.

Instead of going in, Val slipped between the two rows of quilts closest to the house and worked her way slowly down to the end of the porch close to the Flower Power truck.

"You need help bringing in the flowers, ma'am?" Ethan asked.

"No, no, they're all in. A lovely young lady helped me. I believe you're engaged to her."

"So Paige beat me to the punch, did she?" Affection and pride were in his voice.

And, Val saw as she reached the end of the quilts and could look around them, in his face.

"She did. You might find she is ahead of you in many things. Do not be afraid to let her lead."

"Ma'am?" Now there was only confusion.

"Where are you from? That accent…?"

"North Carolina, ma'am. Blue Ridge Mountains. Do you know the area?"

"Not at all, except… Yes. Yes, that's it exactly. You must have trillium near where you live."

"Trillium?"

Ethan clearly had no idea what it was. Neither did Val, but she had a suspicion.

Myrtha was muttering to herself, then finally responded to Ethan. "Yes, trillium. Grows in the wild, covers quite an area of the continent. Most often white blooms. Quite pretty. But that doesn't mean you can pick it. Not ever. If you pick the flower it will die. Do not pick it in the wild for any reason," she said severely, staring at him.

"I, uh, won't."

"Good." Her manner relaxed. "But you can buy the bulbs. If you can find a plant, that would be best, because it would take a couple years to cultivate it properly, so don't wait for that this time. Several Native American tribes used it medicinally. It's been used for dysentery, earache, as a poultice on the skin for ulcers and if there was concern about gangrene, but most of all it was used to help with childbirth. Some call it birthroot. It was sacred to women. Do you know what it looks like?"

"No." It sounded as if he'd started to say *no clue*, then thought better of it.

"Three leaves, three petals, three sepals."

Val would bet Ethan didn't know what a sepal was, but no way was he going to try to stop Myrtha.

Flower power, all right.

"Three. Do you understand?"

"Three," he repeated.

"Remember that." She opened the truck door. "It blooms April to June, but I would say the end of April. Remember that, too."

"Uh, okay. But ma'am, you said you needed help. What can I help you with?"

She got in the van, looking out at him through the open window. "Oh, you've helped. I just hope *I* have helped enough. Good-bye, young man. Let the trillium help you."

For a moment Ethan watched the truck drive away, then he shrugged and headed back toward the corral past the barn.

Val held her spot until he reached the barn. Partway back down the line of quilts she found her way blocked by Taylor, with Matty right behind her.

"What was that all about?" Taylor asked.

"You were listening?"

"Of course we were listening," Matty said. "Like you."

"I think Myrtha gave Ethan a hint to help him in childbirth." She giggled, feeling relieved. Myrtha's portents about larkspur had gotten under her skin. But if she was advising Ethan about trillium— birthroot—how seriously could she be taken?

She was a lovely woman, but...

Neither Matty nor Taylor joined her amusement. In fact, Taylor frowned.

"What?" Val asked her, pushing back a breeze-swelled quilt of orange and blues to see her better.

"There is something about that woman."

Matty nodded in agreement.

"C'mon, you guys. I know she's a little kooky, but she's really very nice," Val said.

"She *is* nice. It's not that... I told you when Jack brought you yellow monkeyflower last summer, how there have been wildflowers associated with a lot of the couples around here. Did you know the guys took Matt to the Flower Power shop a while back when he and Zoe were dancing around each other without ever getting any closer?"

"No, I didn't. Jack was part of that, too?"

"Yup. And then, lo and behold, Matt transplants a threadleaf phacelia to right in front of his house. That one you took the gorgeous close-up photo of."

She looked over her shoulder to Matty, who picked up, saying, "You know he had it blown up and framed, and then gave it to Zoe."

"When?" Val asked. "Because it wasn't until the flood…"

"I know," Taylor said, "but that flower was part of what brought them together. I just know it. Yes, go ahead, look at me like that. Laugh about a hard-headed lawyer being fanciful, but I know I'm right."

Val chewed at her lip. "Matty?"

She shook her head. "I'm not laughing. I once asked Dave about my wedding bouquet. Remember it, Taylor?"

"Oh, yes. Indian paintbrush. Unexpected. What about it?"

"Well, Dave got it for me, because I wasn't expecting to have a real wedding. And when I asked him later how he'd come to have a bouquet of Indian paintbrush, he said he got it from a shop across the street from the courthouse and that the woman there helped him figure it out."

"Across from the courthouse?" Taylor repeated. "That's Flower Power. Myrtha's shop. She must be the woman. I knew it. It's all connected."

"What are you girls doing out here?" Irene's head poked around a quilt separating them from the kitchen door.

"Uh, checking the quilts. Seeing if they got damp," Matty said.

Donna's voice came from past Irene. "When would they have gotten damp? That's why we took them in last night."

"And it worked." Matty's upbeat voice clashed with the grimaces she made to Taylor and Val, keeping her back to Irene. "Did you need us?"

"Lucy says she needs Val. She's going to start on the brownies and wants to be sure there's enough chocolate."

"Chocolate," breathed Matty, Taylor, and Val in unison.

"We're coming right now," Taylor added.

But when Val, the last one, cleared the quilts, she stopped abruptly. "Now, what's that they've got?"

She pointed to where Dax and Ethan held a pair of old wooden doors hinged together and braced to stand nearly upright. Rows of hooks marched across the handsome weathered wood.

Donna looked at Irene. Both women smiled without answering.

Not far from the bottom of the steps, Ted was consulting with Dave, who saw his wife at that moment and called to her.

"Be right back," she said as she started down the steps to the men. "Don't hold up the brownie production for me."

"Okay, I can see they're doors," Val said, "but—Oh, is this what Matty asked you if you'd brought, Irene?"

"Yes, it is."

"What's it for?"

Irene patted her shoulder. "You'll see."

"I know I said Matty could surprise me with things at the reception and that means I shouldn't be asking all the time, but this is small, so…"

Donna patted her arm. "Patience, dear."

Val rolled her eyes. "Like I have any of that."

They all laughed. But the laughter didn't soften the older women's resolve when Val tried again with a "Donna?"

"No."

"It will be a nice surprise come Saturday night," Irene promised.

"And in the meantime, there are brownies," Taylor pointed out.

"Good point." Val led the way into the kitchen.

Planning the Wedding:
The Wedding Dress

"I'll just wear one of my regular dresses," Val told her cousin Eleanor on the phone.

"You will not."

"I'm going to be even more pregnant than I am now. Six months. I'll look like a watermelon."

"You're hardly showing a bump in that picture you sent two days ago."

"A bump on a midget like me looks like a watermelon," she said morosely.

"That's hormones talking, Val. You look gorgeous and happy. And you'll look even more gorgeous and happy on that day. If I were there, I'd take you out shopping the way you did for me."

"*Took* you shopping? Make that physically dragged you out. You were going to wear that old silk suit of yours, for heaven's sake. Aren't you glad you didn't? Wasn't I right to drag you out?"

"I am glad. You were right. And you'll be glad and I'll be right to insist you get a proper wedding dress."

"There's not a whole lot of choices out here, El. Besides, it's going to be a really, really casual wedding."

"Don't worry about a thing. I'll take care of it."

Ten days later Donna asked Valerie to come over to the Slash-C for lunch "and plan to stay the afternoon."

When she arrived, the compact living room of Donna and Ed's house was stacked with boxes, half of them opened, with

Taylor hanging the contents on a temporary clothes rack, while Matty worked on opening the second half.

Val stopped abruptly. "What on earth?"

"*This* is your wedding dress store," Donna said. "Eleanor had these selections sent out to you. Matty and Taylor and I are going to assist you trying them on, then send back the ones that don't work."

"And I'm consulting long distance," Eleanor's voice said from the computer.

"Oh, I like this one for you, Val," Taylor said, holding up a sleek, strapless gown.

"Let's start with that one," Matty said.

But first El had another instruction, "You have to stop crying, Val. You'll drip on the dresses."

CHAPTER TWELVE

Paige and Hannah folded napkins for the rehearsal dinner and the wedding. They placed each gently in appropriately labeled boxes, so they would only need a little fluffing when they were set on the tables.

Then—finally—Paige was able to slip away. She half expected to find Ethan in their room, blocking her attempt to research the items on her list—it had been that kind of day so far—but it was empty.

She quickly read the results from her online search with skepticism, which was bolstered by the skepticism of all the experts who said that women who said they knew for sure they were pregnant well before time to take the test were simply misguided, that these tales weren't including all the women who were sure and then proved not to be pregnant.

Good point.

Then she noticed that all the *experts* saying this were men.

Hmm.

She re-tried her search, juggling the terms. She immediately recognized Val's hugely successful mommy blog as the first result to come up.

Posters listed symptoms they'd noticed before a positive pregnancy test that they hadn't noticed other times.

Bleeding gums.

Nope.

Cramping.

Well, yes, but connected to the food poisoning.

Are you sure it was food poisoning? Hannah's voice came in to her head.

Throwing up.

Yup, but that was food poisoning. *Are you sure…?* That circle could go round and round forever.

Sharp little pains in the belly.

Oh. That's what had made her suspect food poisoning, because it was unlike a usual upset stomach.

Tired.

You're taking a nap? Again? You never take naps. But she was on vacation. Who could blame her for a nap? A couple, maybe a few naps.

Cranky.

She was not cra—

I thought you wanted to come to this wedding? If you didn't, you should have spoken up and I'd have held out, no matter what Hannah and Mandy said.

Okay, Ethan might say she was cranky. But everyone got testy sometimes, even with the person they loved. That didn't mean anything.

Sore breasts.

Ummm. Yeah. The shoulder bag strap bothering her. Not her shoulders, her breasts.

Darkened area around the nipples.

She sat straight at that.

All these other so-called symptoms were subjective, open to interpretation, and could easily stem from other causes.

But not this.

She searched for more information. Some sites said this wouldn't happen, if it happened at all, until her cycle was supposed to start. She wasn't quite there yet, so...

But several women on Val's blog and elsewhere said it changed almost immediately for them. A few left out the *almost.*

Paige went to stand in front of the bathroom mirror. She thought she'd be able to see, especially if she stood on her toes.

She pulled up the bottom of her t-shirt. It wouldn't stay up, so she tucked it under her chin, then lowered the front of her bra.

Needing to stand on her toes, plus trying to look up toward the mirror while she had her chin tucked to hold the shirt up, did not provide a clear view. She tried hopping up, to see better, but the bra snapped back into place.

This time, she held the shirt against her throat with one hand, lowered the bra with the other and tried to brace against the front of the sink to keep on tippy-toes balance.

Was that darkening around the left nipple? Or was it the angle? There was a shadow across her right side that made it hard to tell if—

"What are you doing?"

She gasped at Ethan's voice coming from behind her. In the mirror, she saw him leaning against the doorjamb in the bathroom doorway. How in the world had he come in without her hearing him?

"Nothing. Nothing."

Should she tell him?

Tell him what?

She didn't know anything, not for sure.

She yanked the bra up. Now—of course—the t-shirt stayed raised of its own accord.

"Hey, I liked it like that."

One stride into the tiny bathroom brought him up against her back. He put one arm around her waist and used the opposite hand to hold back her hair as he leaned down and kissed the side of her throat.

She tipped her head to give him better access.

His hand at her waist rose, cupping one breast through the fabric.

Then he pulled the bra down—sure, he had no trouble keeping it down. Not that she was complaining, as he stroked each of her breasts in turn, the gentle slide of his palms and fingers with a hint of friction, making her nipples hard, while her knees went soft.

But she forced herself not to sag back against him. In fact, the opposite as she rose up on her toes again. With the shirt up and the bra down ... but his large hand covered where she might have seen a potential early indication of—

She broke off the thought, feeling superstitious.

Besides, it might not be there at all.

And if it was... No. She wouldn't jump that gun. She couldn't.

She slowly let her heels come down, not realizing until it was happening how she rubbed against Ethan as she did.

When she did realize it, she slowed down more, drawing out the delicious sensations.

He groaned in pleasure, then asked, "Do you want to…?"

She did want to. She really did. Perhaps even more, she wanted him to hold her, to be close to her.

"Ethan…" He kissed her neck again, and her next words had all the regret she felt in them. "We can't. They're next door…"

Foiled for a moment, but then his eyes grinned first. "I could use a shower."

"A shower? But you took one—

"Another shower. All that work stringing lights, setting up the kids' rodeo. How about you? In the mood for a shower?"

"Oh. *Oh.* That might do it. That might do it, with lots of loud, running water."

"Lots and lots of loud, running water. For a long, long time."

Paige urged Ethan to go ahead without her. She'd be at the kids' rodeo in a minute.

As soon as the door closed on his departure, she took off her blouse, unhooked her bra and let it drop. She looked down.

She couldn't be sure. Not a hundred percent. It could be the angle. Or the lighting.

Then she got the hand mirror from her purse. She should have thought of this before.

Not angle, not lighting. The areolas were definitely darker.

She squinted. Were they bigger, too? Yes.

She stared a moment longer, let out a long breath, then put her bra and shirt back on.

She looked at herself in the mirror again.

She was pregnant—*might* be pregnant—entirely unexpectedly with the baby of the man she loved and who loved her.

The man with the plan.

The man who scheduled and organized and prepared.

Especially for something as big, as life-changing as a baby.

He'd had those tendencies from the time she'd met him as a boy.

They'd gotten to know each other when they'd been assigned to the same school project. He, of course, had organized the whole thing. Then he'd helped her organize another school assignment. Then a charity project she was part of. When he took over the drive to fund a trip to Washington, D.C., for the middle school to be in a parade, it topped its goal easily.

So she knew it was simply part of his personality.

Then Mr. and Mrs. Chalmers—no matter how old she got, they would always be frozen as the adults she knew as a child, always Mr. and Mrs. Chalmers—were killed in that small plane crash outside of Atlanta.

A part failed, the final report she'd read for the first time a few years ago said. It also said they had purposely moved away from populated areas when they realized the severity of the issue. That delayed finding the wreck and their bodies, while it spared other lives.

Ethan had changed with their deaths. Mandy, too. Not a sudden reversal of who they were, but for each, a deepening, hardening of previous tendencies.

Before their parents' deaths it was like they'd been riding along on different but parallel tracks, within arm's reach of each other.

After, those tracks diverged, leading them ever farther away from each other. That was when the twin tiffs began.

The man with the plan for everything. Never bothering to live.

He hadn't planned for this. Neither of them had.

Could you plan for a miracle?

Because her becoming pregnant without trying was—would be, if it was true—practically a miracle.

An unscheduled miracle.

How on earth was Ethan going to take that?

Planning the Wedding:

The Music

Jack came up behind her where she was answering comments on her blog.

He'd wandered down the hall as if going to their bedroom, but she'd heard the telltale squeak and knew he'd checked in on Addie, as he did about this time every night and again when they went together to her room before they went to bed.

He waited for her to stop typing, then bent, swept her hair aside and kissed her shoulder.

"I have an idea for the wedding," he said.

Hard to say which she liked more—the kiss or that he was joining in more and more.

Still, she couldn't resist teasing him. Besides, it was good for him. He still tended toward being too solemn.

"Something other than forgetting all this and eloping immediately."

He chuckled quietly. "Yeah. Let's say a second choice after that."

"Okay, let's hear it."

"Cahill."

"Cahill? What about him?"

"His music. Heard the end of those songs he recorded for Addie to go to sleep to, and I thought what could be better? Not lullabies, but Cahill playing. Maybe singing. Him and his guitar."

She pivoted toward him, catching his hand in both of hers. "That is brilliant. *You* are brilliant. Absolutely brilliant. We'll have to figure out which songs and we'll need to spell him so he can eat and dance and celebrate, but especially for the ceremony, nothing could be better."

"What are you doing?"

"Calling to ask if he'll do it."

"It's late there."

"I'll just see if he's online."

He was.

"You ask him," Val told Jack.

After he did, in a minimal number of words, Cahill said he'd be honored.

Eleanor came on in the background, beaming her approval.

Then they began the discussion of which songs would be played when. Until Cahill and Val had so many possibilities that Cahill declared it would be the first wedding ceremony that lasted an entire summer and he'd have no voice or finger-tips left by the end.

Jack and Val, with a solitary assist from Addie ("Don't like that one,") brought the choices down to a reasonable list.

Then they came up with a surprise for the reception that would involve only them, Jack, Kiernan, and possibly two more.

Val almost laughed to see that nearly everyone was on-hand when Kiernan returned from going to the airport to pick up his girlfriend.

He made the introductions with pride and Felicity received them with charm.

Since Kiernan had introduced her to Val first, that left her free to observe the rest.

El and Cahill were there, of course. And it made sense that some of the Trimarco clan Felicity had met before would say hello and make her welcome.

But the Wyoming side of the wedding party and guests was well represented, too—everyone except Paige, Dave, and Jack—and that was probably mostly curiosity.

She considered that. Curiosity and perhaps a bit of protectiveness.

Strange how Kiernan had become part of the group so quickly.

Or was she projecting her own thoughts, thinking the others were being protective?

And, really, why would they be?

Some mumbo-jumbo about larkspur?

What was the matter with her getting all tied in knots about that? Yes, the woman's eyes were amazingly like the color of her mother's delphiniums, also known as larkspur. And, yes, larkspur was not good for a cattle ranch. But, come on.

Her hormones were getting completely out of hand to think this nice woman posed a threat.

Might she hurt Kiernan? Yes. Or vice versa.

From behind her, she heard Ethan's voice, saying, "Here you are. I was beginning to wonder—Hey, are you okay?"

She turned and saw that Paige had joined the outside of the group. And past her, Dave was approaching from the direction of the corral.

"I'm fine, Ethan."

"Your eyes are red. Have you—You weren't crying were you?"

"I must have gotten some soap or shampoo in my eyes."

"Sorry about that." He grinned and she did, too.

Val stifled her own grin. Not hard to guess what those two had been up to. Had that been why Paige had wanted to slip away before? Sure couldn't blame them. She wouldn't mind some more alone time with Jack, either.

But then Ethan's grin faded. "Are you sure…?"

"I'm sure. I have no reason to cry. No reason at all."

"Ah, Paige," Kiernan said, "come here and meet Felicity. Felicity, this is Ethan's fiancée we were telling you about." Kiernan added, as Dave came up, "And this is Dave Currick, one of the owners of the Slash-C."

"Thank you for not leading with me being Matty's husband," he said dryly. "It's—"

"That was already covered," Kiernan said, while the rest chuckled.

"—a pleasure to meet *you*, Felicity." His emphasis teased that her boyfriend wasn't such a pleasure.

"Felicity Roberts," Kiernan confirmed.

"Roberts? That's my mom's maiden name," Dave said. "Maybe you're related, which would mean we're related, so—"

"No."

The flatness of Felicity's single word was a sour note thrown into the mood of harmony, but sometimes a word came out wrong.

Felicity obviously recognized it, because she flushed and quickly said, "I mean, it's such a common name. And I know our family tree pretty well. I definitely would have noticed someone living on a ranch in Wyoming, because I would have been on your doorstep in my youthful horse-crazy phase."

Val looked around at the other faces and saw that Felicity had pulled off easing everyone past that awkward flat note.

"I got stuck in that phase," Matty said cheerfully.

"And I've only discovered it in the past year," Val added.

"Too bad you missed the ranch tour yesterday, Felicity." Kiernan's eyes glinted with teasing. "All on horseback, it was."

She groaned. "Rub it in, McCrea. Rub it in."

They looked at each other for a moment, and Val's heart lifted. *Oh, yes, this will work out for Kiernan.*

Felicity broke the look and turned to her. "Your fiancé's not here?"

"Oh, he will be. He's preparing for a new horse. One of his friends—" She loved saying that and nudging him none too gently to also say it. "—who's coming for the wedding had heard about a horse being abused, so he's bringing it for Jack."

"An abused horse?"

Val smiled at her astonishment. "Yup."

"Don't people usually bring, uh, blenders or silver fish forks and such as presents?"

She laughed. "We have a blender and would have no idea what to do with silver fish forks."

"That's right," Kiernan said, "you never saw their invitation. Val and Jack were vehement about no gifts."

"Except abused horses?" Felicity asked.

"Exactly. Jack works wonders with them."

"He does?"

This time the younger woman's surprise sounded different, though Val couldn't pinpoint the difference.

"He sure does," Matty confirmed.

"Has quite the reputation for it around the region," Dave said. He tipped his head toward Dax. "And a good amount of help from a network of ranchers around."

"Couldn't happen without the support here at the Slash-C," Dax said.

As the two men explained what Jack did in response to questions from Felicity, all the while trying to sidestep any credit for their own roles, Val's thoughts went to Jack.

A new horse to help was what he needed amid all the sociability of this wedding weekend.

He was making great progress in recognizing that he *was* connected to people, that many cared about him. But she wasn't foolish enough to expect him to turn into a party guy.

He still needed plenty of time alone. Except for a thousand pounds of horseflesh that wanted nothing to do with him. Perfect company for Jack Ralston.

While Jack sat in the corral with the horse hour after hour, appearing not to be paying any heed to the animal, he learned so much.

All information he'd use once the horse started to accept him, and then that wonderful moment when its curiosity overcame all that it had been put through and it ventured close to Jack, beginning their partnership.

Hey, whatever soothed your soul.

Bubble baths worked for some. For the man she'd fallen in love with it was being still and silent until a traumatized horse got used to him. Then, slowly adding in movement and sound.

Though never too much talking.

That was her role in the relationship.

"What are you smiling at, Val?" Kiernan's question brought her back to the moment.

"Sorry. What were you saying?"

"Not me, Felicity."

"I was asking if we can watch your fiancé with the horse when it arrives."

"Sorry, no. The fewer people around, the less activity the better. He likes to keep everything as quiet and calm as possible."

"In the opposite of quiet and calm, we'll be starting the kids' rodeo soon," Matty said.

"But first," Dave said in time with a shuddering clap of thunder, "we'll have a brief delay while we all run for cover in the barn!"

CHAPTER THIRTEEN

Ethan protected her from the worst of the gush of rain as they ran to the barn, while he also made way for Irene and Donna and Lucy and Jimmy Trimarco to get in to the shelter ahead of them.

As they shook the rain off, Paige caught movement from the corner of her eye and saw Kiernan and Felicity by themselves, near some of the stacked hay bales.

Their laughter faded as they looked into each other's eyes.

Paige thought she could feel the heat from where she stood.

Kiernan took off his cowboy hat and leaned in. They were kissing as they dropped from sight below the level of the hay bale.

For an instant she imagined she could see steam rising from the spot.

"Looks like we've got some escapees," Ethan said from beside her.

But he wasn't looking toward where Kiernan and Felicity had disappeared.

He was watching Val, Eleanor, and Cahill exit a door at the far end of the barn, into the rain.

Val had led El and Cahill to this spot.

They were well above the corral, out of the horse's line of sight, and wearing camouflage ponchos that they'd belted to keep them from flapping in the wind.

Jack had set up panels earlier to create a chute that would direct the horse into the round corral.

Walker Riley expertly backed the horse trailer into place, with Jack and Dax directing him in.

Walker and Matt Halderman exited the cab, meeting with Jack and Dax for several minutes of conversation.

"They'll be talking about how this horse loads and unloads. Some of the horses are completely passive, but from what Walker has told Jack, this one's more aggressive."

"Aggressive?" El sounded apprehensive.

"Kicking, biting."

"Oh, dear."

"They know how to handle him," Cahill said.

The consultation broke up. Walker went to the front of the trailer, Matt and Dax to the back and Jack to the center of the corral.

Cahill made a sound. "What?" El asked, looking from one to the other.

"Jack's saying it's his space. Right from the start," Cahill said.

"Exactly. Oh, they brought his paddock buddy," Val added as Dax swung open the solid gate of the trailer and they could see two horses angled inside.

"His what?"

"Horses are herd animals," Val said, sharing what Jack had taught her. "They don't like to be alone. This might make it easier on him."

The paddock buddy unloaded himself, wandering over to Jack to check him out. Jack held his position, made the horse wait a moment, then rubbed his nose.

"Ready," he said in a low voice.

Matt went in to the trailer, swinging the second gate so it protected him from the horse. Even so, the horse made a move toward him before he turned and exited the trailer.

El sucked in a breath. "He's gorgeous."

"He is that," Cahill agreed.

The horse cut the distance to Jack in half and reared. Jack stayed still. The horse tossed his head twice, then finally broke to one side, trotting over to his paddock buddy.

"Gorgeous and trouble on four legs," Cahill said.

Dave strode across the corral to the audience.

The spectators' seats were mostly the top rail of the corral fence, though a couple pickups were backed up to the fence, the beds outfitted with chairs and steps to reach them, for those who preferred that seating.

"Ladies and gentlemen," Dave intoned, quieting the chatter, "welcome to the Jack and Val wedding kids' rodeo. We hope the rodeo experts in the crowd will guide the newcomers through the intricacies of our demanding sport, where skill is as necessary as courage."

"Val?" came her mother's concerned voice.

Donna patted Lucy's arm. "It's okay. That's my son being dramatic."

"Mo-om," Dave protested.

It was mostly drowned out by laughter.

"Best get on with the show," suggested Ed Currick.

More laughter came as Dave cleared his throat, took off his cowboy hat, and said, "And now, on with the show," as he bowed and touched the soft dirt with the sweep of his hat.

He took up a spot between two of the fence-sitters and said loudly, "Our first event today is the highly technical Sheep Scramble."

He waved his hat over his head as a signal. A gate opened at the far side of the corral and a single young sheep with a green ribbon around its tail ambled a yard into the corral and stopped, gazing around.

Another gate opened, revealing a knot of kids. A few of the older boys were poised in the forward-leaning standing start position runners once used. The rest of the kids milled around.

"Ready, set, go!" shouted Jack.

Most of the kids took off, with Cal, Dax, and Bryan behind them, but Matty was seen coaxing Taylor and Cal's youngest to enter the corral.

In the meantime, the lead group had nearly reached the sheep. It watched them approach placidly, until one of the boys, who'd moved to come around behind it, closed the gap to a couple feet, then it loped away.

The kids streamed after it as the maneuver was repeated two more times, while the spectators cheered and laughed.

Taylor and Cal's son Rob had stopped about ten feet into the arena, pointing up at a bird. The sheep, keeping track of the pursuers, closed in on the boy.

A new figure streaked past into the corral, putting itself between the sheep and the child.

It was Cal and Taylor's collie, Sin. He barked at the sheep, which came to a full stop, as Cal scooped up the child to his delight, judging by the squeals of "Higher, higher."

With the kids closing in, the sheep went sideways, escaping again.

But the kids now had an ally, because Sin had sized up the situation. The dog got in front of the sheep again and crouched, holding the other animal in place with the force of its stare.

That let the kids catch up. Brennan was first to reach the sheep, untied the ribbon, and triumphantly held it aloft.

Cal and Dax started to shoo the kids toward their gate, while Bryan went after the sheep. But Sin was still on the job, escorting the sheep to his gate, then gathering up the last of the kids to wild applause from the audience.

Jack, Cal, and Dax came in with barrels, spacing them out in a triangle in the corral.

Felicity leaned around Kiernan to ask Val, "Is one of the helpers over there your fiancé?"

Val pointed. "That's Jack. Next to his friend—and groomsman— Dax Randall. You met Dax earlier. And that's Walker Riley and Matt Halderman—Matt's in the blue shirt. They're both former rodeo cowboys. Walker still runs a rodeo in Park, Wyoming with his wife, Kalli, and Matt's not far from here now with a place for retired rodeo animals. You'll meet all of them and Matt's girlfriend, Zoe Parisi, at the wedding."

"So they were able to leave the new horse long enough to do this?"

Val couldn't detect any edge in those words. She forced any out of her response, making it a simple, cheerful, "Yup."

"Will he be able to join us for dinner? The groom, I mean."

"Hey, I'm going to start getting jealous here. He is engaged to Val, you know," Kiernan said.

Everyone laughed.

"So what about you two?" Lucy Trimarco asked.

Color came up Felicity's throat and into her cheeks, which said she'd understood the question perfectly. Still, she tried to deflect it. "The two of us? We'll be staying for the wedding, then—"

"She means a future for you two, you and Kiernan. You know, commitment, living together, marriage."

Eleanor issued a warning with a low, "Val."

"I know, I know. I am my mother." She laughed, joined by others.

But she'd also noticed Kiernan's reaction. He'd wanted to hear an answer to those questions, too.

Dave spoke up again in his announcer's voice. "For our next event, Stick Pony barrel racing—the upper division."

The older kids came out with stick ponies and took turns running from barrel to barrel, circling each one, before racing to the finish line.

The barrels were moved closer together for the "lower division." The little ones mostly wandered from barrel to barrel with a lot of coaching and coaxing from the three men to get them around each one.

Finn Currick took a detour from her route to approach the fence in order to say hello to everyone, while Bobby Trimarco's youngest stopped to retie the bandana around his mount's "neck."

"Hey, Dave," called out Anthony Trimarco. "Noticed you had the events with the kids running around at the start. Getting them all worn out, huh?"

"You bet. This ain't my first rodeo."

That drew lots of laughter.

The next event was Stick Pony Pole Bending races.

The men set up white poles weighted at the bottom in a line with six-foot gaps between them. The kids came out one by one on their stick ponies, weaving around the poles, going up the corral, then turning and doing the same thing down the corral.

With that competition complete, Dave announced they were about to enjoy an impressive demonstration.

In a momentary lull, the breeze brought Brennan Currick's young voice from the far side of the corral, demanding, "Why does she get to go last? I'm a better rider than her."

"N'huh-huh," came Addie's voice. "Besides, I'm getting married with Mom and Daddy Jack. You're not."

"Mo-om." Brennan's protest was such a close approximation of his father's earlier that everyone laughed again.

"Helmet on or you're not going at all," Matty said.

Everyone who'd been helping except Matty came out and either side of the pole course. Cal and Taylor's Cassie came out first on a little pony, and successfully negotiated the poles at a sedate pace. Brennan tried to holler up some speed from an animal who thought plodding might break the sound barrier. Next, a neighbor boy also tried going faster, but his mount had other ideas, stopping dead and needing significant encouragement from Bryan's cowboy hat to restart.

Addie was last, as advertised.

Her ride wasn't so much a race as a royal progression. Each time the weaving pattern between the poles brought horse and rider closer to her audience, she waved and called hellos, with Buster accommodating this by leaving the route and heading toward the spectators. Dax and Matt Halderman had to redirect the horse.

As Addie and Buster slowly reached the gate where Matty waited, Dave said, "And finally, we'd like to show you how these kids will be doing this in a few years. Jack?"

Jack looked up from where he held two of the poles, clearly surprised.

"Oh, yes, please, Jack?" Val called out.

"C'mon," Dave urged. "Show your in-laws-to-be what you can do."

"Storm's not saddled," he protested.

"Yes, he is," Bryan said with a grin, taking one of the poles from him.

The other men in the corral encouraged him as they set the poles farther apart, measuring the distance between as they went.

Jack met Val's gaze across the space. She nodded.

He raised his hand in acknowledgement and headed for the gate.

"Storm's one of the abused horses Jack's worked with." The explanation was mostly for Felicity, since the others had already heard that and more.

"But how does he know how to do that?"

Felicity sounded more disbelieving that surprised, but Val figured that was because it was such a foreign concept to the Easterner.

Then she had to stifle a laugh at herself for the thought, since she'd been the ultimate Easterner before last summer. Before Jack.

"He taught himself." Val heard the pride in her voice, and caught several smiles directed her way. "He's read a lot. Talked to people. Took workshops. But I think mostly it's him watching and listening to the horse. And thinking how he'd react in their situation and what might make them turn around their lives after being treated rough."

"Ready," came Dax's shout from across the corral.

Storm danced a bit beyond the open gate on that side of the corral. Then, in an instant, the horse jumped forward and was racing to the far end of the poles, turning and weaving between them to the opposite end, where another tight turn started horse and rider back through the poles. A final turn and they raced back alongside the line of poles and out the gate.

"That was amazing," Mandy said, standing to applaud, along with most of the rest of the spectators. "Boy, I'd like to learn to do that."

"It's a lot harder than it looks," Dave said. "Storm's a pretty special horse. Some horses are quick in the turns, some are fast in the straightaways. Storm's both."

"And Jack's a great rider," Val said.

Dave grinned at her. "He is that."

"Well, this has been fun," Lucy said. "I don't know why you were worried, Val. Now, back to you two," she added as an introduction to peppering Felicity about her relationship with Kiernan and its possible future.

Val noticed the young woman was quite adroit at noncommittal answers.

She also noticed who hadn't objected to the talk about their possible future.

It sure looked like Kiernan McCrea had been hooked at last. She'd have expected that thought to bring a grin.

It didn't.

Planning the Wedding:

The Seating Plan

"I like the thing where people mix together. You know, sitting on whichever side they feel like, instead of people for the bride on one side and the groom on the other. I don't like that. I've been to too many weddings where I knew both people and had no idea which side to choose. And then there are the ones where it's totally lopsided and I hate that."

"We can do that. No problem." Matty made a note. Then she clicked on her device. "What do you think of something like this for seating during the ceremony?"

"Are those… They're hay bales, aren't they? And what's on top?"

"Hay bales with quilts covering them. The quilts will keep them from being itchy. But we could rent chairs if you don't like it."

"I love it. It's perfect. Absolutely perfect. So colorful. And after the wedding, we can use the hay up, right?"

"Absolutely. Great recycling."

"But all those quilts we'd need—"

"Won't be an issue. We'll put out the call around here and there'll be a stampede. We'll have more than we could possibly use. We'll have to be diplomatic about—What? I see that look.

You have an idea."

She grinned. "Is there any reason the bales have to be lined up like church pews?"

"Not that I can think of." Matty clicked to another photo. "They can be ringed around the altar instead of lined up in rows."

"Mmm."

"I see that brain working. What do you have in mind, Val?"

"What if there's no center aisle? Set them up so they zigzag. People would have to sort of wander to find seats, pass other people, maybe chat…What do you think?"

"I think it's brilliant."

Ethan was not alone in being reluctant to try the line dancing that night, but Val succeeded in rounding up not only the neophytes but also a fair number of the experienced dancers.

Lisa, Taylor, and Zoe stood in front, prepared to demonstrate.

"How'd Jack get a pass on this?" Anthony demanded.

"He knows how to dance already."

"What about you, Val?" Anthony pursued.

"I already know how to do this and I'm needed to DJ."

"You're going to do that Saturday night, too?"

"No-oo," she drew it out in sibling mockery. "I'm going to be otherwise occupied."

"We'll start with a few core steps," Lisa said, "then—"

"Are we too late?" Lucy, Donna, and Irene came hurrying up from inside.

"Mom?" Val questioned. "Are you going to—? I mean, Donna danced with a Broadway tour, but—"

"That was so long ago, dear, it hardly counts."

But Val had seen Donna dance, as well as ride and work around the ranch. She was trim and in shape. Not to mention she could *move*.

Her mom was a wizard in the kitchen, but on the dance floor?

"I will have you know I was a champion step-dancer as a girl."

Val felt her jaw dropping and snapped it up. "You were? But you're not Irish."

"I have a touch. And in Gloucester at that time there weren't ballet lessons or gymnastics or any of that. There was step-dancing. These line dances of yours can't be too different."

"I'm sure you're right," Donna said.

Against that united front, no one was foolish enough to question more.

They made room in the front row for them.

"We'll start with the grapevine, a fundamental step that shows up in lots of dances. Step to the right, step behind, step…"

Grapevines grew with twists and turns, then there were bumps, hitches, boogies, kicks, claps, and boot slaps. They started with the Cupid Shuffle, went on to the Electric Slide, the Tush Push, then the Cowboy Boogie.

There were laughs, groans, and a fair amount of "Go, Mrs. T's!"

At the end, everyone collapsed to the nearest sittable surface.

Val reached over to put her hand on her mother's shoulder. "You were amazing, Mom."

"Thank you, dear. It's been a long, long time. But the basics were coming back to me. I'll be better at the reception."

"There'll be some harder dances then," Val warned.

"Holy moly," Anthony said between his remaining pants. "There's more than we've done?"

"Just scratching the surface," his sister said with relish. "Wait until you see the best dancers do Footloose on Saturday night. Even when I'm not pregnant I can't keep up with that. There are lots and lots more advanced dances. Harder *and* faster."

He groaned. Everyone else laughed.

"We'll all sleep well tonight."

CHAPTER FOURTEEN

FRIDAY

Paige had left Ethan sleeping soundly.

It was early, no one else was around as she searched for the unfamiliar rental car among all the trucks and four-wheel-drives. When she did find it, she also found a problem.

"Did you want to go somewhere, Paige?"

She spun around to face Donna Currick. So much for no one else being around.

"I was going to go into town on an errand."

Donna looked over the situation. "Your rental car's blocked in but good."

She sighed. "Yeah."

"We could rouse a couple of them to move their vehicles and get you out." Donna eyed the arrangement of vehicles. "Maybe four of them."

"I don't want to disturb anyone… I suppose I could wait and ask Hannah or Dax if I could use their truck later, once people are awake. It's over there on the edge."

The problem was, *people* would include Ethan.

He'd want to know why she wanted to go into town. Possibly would say he'd come with her. And if he didn't, the chances were good Hannah or Mandy would.

And she doubted she'd do well evading them or their questions.

"No need to disturb a soul," Donna said. "I was about to drive into town myself. You come on with me right now."

"I couldn't—"

"Oh, I'll make you work for your trip," Donna said with a smile. "I could use a hand at my last stop. C'mon, in you go."

She didn't ask until they were near town where Paige wanted to go.

"A pharmacy? I had a bout of food poisoning a few days ago and I'm still feeling poorly."

"Hannah mentioned that had hit you during the trip here. How miserable."

"It wasn't as bad as it could have been. It didn't hit while we were on the plane. I didn't have to contend with that. I, uh, just want to shake the last of it."

"I'm sure you'll find something at Van Hopft's. If you wouldn't mind, I'll drop you off and you could pick up a few things for me, too. Want to make sure we don't run out over the weekend. Then we'll meet for a little breakfast at the café."

"Oh, no, I don't think—"

"Rainie at the café would never forgive me if we didn't stop by."

Paige could not have planned it better.

The items from Donna's list—kids' sunscreen, pain relievers, eye contact solution, and half a dozen more—made the pregnancy test kit just another item to be run up. Without a word, the clerk slid it into its own bag, then dropped it in the bigger bag.

That let Paige transfer it to her purse with no ado, as she walked to the café.

Inside, Donna broke off her chat with the waitress behind the counter to introduce them, then highly recommended the rancher's breakfast. But Paige had smelled pancakes and there was nothing else in the world she could imagine eating at that moment.

A stream of people came by the table to say hello to Donna with every one of them saying they'd see her at the ranch for the wedding the next day.

Paige hardly noticed. She was too busy eating pancakes.

Back at the vehicle, Donna said with a smile, "Now, I'm going to put you to work."

"I hope it's not too strenuous. I am so stuffed from those pancakes I'm not sure I can bend over. I can't remember ever eating that many."

"Mmm-hmm. It often happens that way. Sometimes you can't bear the thought of eating anything. Other times something hits you right and you can't stop."

Paige's head snapped around to her, startled, but also unsure if the older woman had meant what she thought she might have meant.

"Here we are. Stop one," Donna said.

As they went to seven houses around Knighton and picked up freshly cut garden flowers stowed in coolers, in vases set in boxes, wrapped in wet newspapers, and in combinations of the three, Donna said not another word on the subject, while Paige's mind never left it.

With the last pickup safely stowed in the back of the four-wheel-drive, they headed back toward the ranch.

Paige intended to make the drive in silence. Not angry or defensive. Simply dignified silence.

So she was surprised to hear her own voice. "You can't think—I mean it's not what you might think. Or maybe you're not thinking anything at all and I'm making a big deal of... nothing." The last word came out small and sad.

"I *am* thinking, and I suspect it is what I think." Donna focused straight ahead. "I do have some experience, you know. First-hand and observational."

More words burst out of Paige. "You can't—I haven't told Ethan anything. There's no reason to."

Donna glanced at her. "No reason to no matter what the result is?"

"Of course, if... But it won't be. Even if... Well, it would be early. Really, really early, so there's no way. Not to mention that I don't believe I am. The doctors all said over and over that I'd have a really hard time getting pregnant if I could at all. They aren't wrong about things like that."

Another sideways look from Donna. "Don't answer if you don't want to—have you been using protection?"

"We've been so sure—the doctors are so sure—we haven't bothered."

"Ah."

"It wasn't careless. If you heard the doctors…" She heard herself spilling out her medical history, the doctors' pronouncements, Ethan's plans to overcome the obstacle. "So, I can't be. This is to confirm that and shut off these stupid thoughts."

She didn't mention she might also need to show the negative result to Hannah to stop Ethan's sister from having stupid thoughts, too.

Donna's murmur was completely noncommittal.

Paige swung open her vehicle door and climbed out.

"Hey, there. Morning. Where'd you go?"

Ethan.

Oh, God, and she'd never finished her sentence telling—begging—Donna not to mention anything to Ethan.

She tried to make eye contact with the older woman, but Ethan was standing between them.

"I texted you. I went into town with Donna."

If Donna said something now—on purpose or accidentally—there would be no choice but to tell Ethan everything. Immediately. Before she knew one way or the other.

"Yeah, but why?" he asked.

"As a favor to me," Donna said with a smile. "We were the only two around and Paige kindly offered to come with to pick up cut flowers from friends' gardens for the tables tonight."

Ethan put his arm around Paige and kissed the top of her head. "That was nice of you. But *more* flowers?"

"Absolutely more flowers. And now you can help us unload them," Donna said.

Ethan pitched right in.

Paige saw that in addition to soothing her anxiety, Donna's response had eased Ethan's curiosity.

She wouldn't be backed into telling him about the test, about the possible symptoms, about … everything.

The decision was still hers.

She was not at all sure how she felt about that.

But the first priority was to find a quiet moment of privacy to take the test.

When Paige met her eyes, Donna only smiled.

Matty unwittingly prevented Paige from using the kit by asking her to join a group doing the initial setup for tonight's rehearsal dinner.

She considered excusing herself for a while.

But she didn't want to be rushed, because she sure didn't want to mess it up, and she wasn't too sure how long it would take.

Not to mention that Hannah was sure to ask if she was feeling okay.

Nope. Too complicated. She'd wait until she had some time to herself.

Bryan did most of the manual labor of setting up the tables on the patio under a wall-less tent cover. Paige joined Felicity, Hannah, Mandy, Lisa, and Taylor in opening chairs, then dividing up table-cloths, place settings, and decorations for each table. The tables would not be set until much closer to dinner—Wyoming's unpredictable skies and wind made the delay prudent.

They worked steadily, adding the flowers she and Donna had picked up this morning to Ball jars, separating strings of battery operated fairy lights to run down the centers of the tables, arranging everything each table would need on chairs beside it so the final prep would be fast, simple, and organized.

Ethan was involved with a group working on setup for tonight's rehearsal and tomorrow's ceremony by the main barn doors.

The plan was to have the ceremony and spectators outside. But if the weather turned bad, the doors would be closed, bringing the decorations on them to face inside, and the altar would be turned around to the face the open part of the barn, where the audience would be.

He and Dax came over, carrying the heavy wooden doors that Irene and Ted had brought.

"Matty wants these in here now, in the corner by the wedding party's table," Dax said.

While Bryan and Dax moved some of the still folded tables out of the way, Ethan held the doors and chatted easily with the women, informing them lunch, planned early to leave time for everyone to prepare for the late-afternoon rehearsal, would start at any moment.

Job done, he waved as he and Dax headed toward the kitchen.

Felicity said. "Ethan's such a good guy."

She looked up, wondering at a note she couldn't quite pin down in the other woman's voice. The two of them were finishing up a table in one corner, away from the others. "Yes, he is."

"You're lucky. You're so sure of him. He's so sure of you. Nothing could happen to take that away."

Was that true?

She'd thought so.

She hoped so.

But how would he feel if the test said yes?

How would she feel if it said no?

God, she had to take that test. This not knowing had to be worse than not knowing, didn't it?

Right after lunch. Definitely right after lunch.

Paige found a smile. "You aren't doing too shabby, yourself."

Felicity remained solemn. "Kiernan is a wonderful man. He's... He's special." She straightened. "Ah, looks like lunch is ready. Matty's waving to us to come over."

"Hey, am I too late for lunch?"

They were scattered around the porch seats, the steps, and chairs on the patio—staying well away from the tables on pain of extreme displeasure from Matty and the group who'd been working on their set-up.

Val tried not to grin as she turned to new arrival Jack and teased, "What? Did the horse get bored with you?"

"He said I could take a break to see the woman who'll be my fian-cée for only one more day." He kissed her briefly, but satisfyingly, keeping one arm around her. "Also wanted to check in if Matty needs me to do anything this afternoon."

Matty, who'd been running down what remained to be done, immediately said, "You and the rest of the wedding party are to report to the rehearsal at three-thirty in appropriate attire. Other than that, not a thing. Everyone else already knows the drill for this afternoon."

"You might even get more time with your horse," Val said.

"Hey, Dax took us out to that hill to watch what you were doing," Anthony said. "Boy, and they say fishing is boring. If we hadn't seen Storm and some other horses Dave said you'd worked with, I'd say you'd found the best boondoggle ever, sitting out there doing nothing for hours."

"Only to somebody not paying attention," his brother objected. "If you were watching instead of running your mouth—"

"Boys," Lucy reprimanded automatically. "If these others left anything at all, you should go in and get a plate, Jack. But I think Kiernan has an introduction to make first."

"I do," Kiernan said, clearly proud and pleased to make this introduction, and his girlfriend. "I'd like you to meet Felicity Roberts. Felicity, this is Jack Ralston.

Val saw the lines around Jack's eyes deepen slightly in an anticipatory smile as he turned away from her so he could face Kiernan.

Jack froze.

Suddenly and completely. Val felt it in his arm around her, in his body beside her.

Not able to see his face, she automatically looked to the faces she could see for an explanation.

Everyone else looked normal.

Except Felicity.

No expression showed on her pretty face at all. Unless the stiffness of concentrated determination was considered an expression.

"Hello, Michael. Sorry—" There was no regret in the word as Felicity spoke it. "—I can't call you Jack."

Jack's arm around Val tightened to a painful band. He drew her back, partially behind him, putting himself between her and Felicity.

"Jack?" He must have heard something in her tone, because he eased his hold on her, though he showed no other sign of recognizing that anyone was there except the young woman facing him.

Val stepped around to she could see his face.

"Oh, God, Jack. What's wrong?"

CHAPTER FIFTEEN

Even as she'd asked what was wrong, Val recognized that this woman who'd come here as Kiernan's girlfriend was something very different to Jack.

She was a piece of his past. The painful past that had finally untwisted from around his heart last summer.

She had to be, using that name and his reaction.

She turned to the younger woman.

There was pain there, too. But also a kind of … satisfaction, even triumph.

Rage flared to life. Bringing this look to Jack's face brought her *satisfaction*? *We'll see about that.* And as for *triumph—*

Val advanced toward her. "Get out. Get out right now."

"Val," Eleanor stepped in.

But it was a touch on her arm that stopped Val from using the fists her hands had become.

Jack's touch.

She spun back to him, clasping his hand.

Without looking at her, he put his free hand over both of theirs, then she covered his, their hands tight and strong.

"Hello, Lis." Jack's voice sounded almost normal, except for a thread of pain. "What are you doing here?"

"What? You didn't want a ghost or the sister of a ghost at your happy wedding?"

"Felicity." Kiernan reached to her.

Other than pulling her arm away, she showed no sign of hearing him. All her attention was on Jack.

Val had some of the pieces now.

Jack had long been suspected in his college girlfriend's disappearance. It had cost him friends. It had cost him the life he'd built. It had cost him her family, which once he'd viewed as his own. His first experience of a true, loving, welcoming family. All gone amid suspicions and grief.

Eventually, he'd come west, finding a life and people who cared about him—as much as he had let them—at the Slash-C. Until last summer, when Val and Addie crashed back into his life.

And then, finally, the answer to Hayley's disappearance.

Her remains, along with those of other young women, had been found in the basement of her cousin's family home.

Jack had been exonerated.

Which did nothing to wipe away the years of loss, sorrow, grief, and isolation. What had done that, finally, was letting himself love and be loved again.

And now, at the celebration of that love, this arrival from the past. This angry, brittle arrival from the past.

"You know he's innocent," she said.

The younger woman didn't look at Val, but Kiernan and the others did. She thought she heard El suck in a breath.

They were figuring it out, too. All those who loved her and Jack. Who'd gone through that time when the story broke last summer. Who knew what he'd gone through.

"Innocent? *Innocent?*" Felicity's voice raised the hairs on the back of Val's neck.

Jack turned and walked away.

"You leave him alone," Val ordered, then followed him.

"What is this, Felicity?" Kiernan demanded, hearing the Irish come strong in his voice. Then it came even stronger. "What the *hell* is this?"

"Don't walk away. I want to talk." She took a step after Jack and Val, focused completely on them. "You owe that to me, Michael."

"He owes it to you, you say? What does that mean?" Kiernan turned her by her shoulders to face him. "Who *are* you?"

She twisted away. When Kiernan would have resumed his hold, Cahill, stepped in, saying something old and soft to him.

But Cahill had also blocked her from going after Jack and Val.

"Who am I? you asked." She turned, pacing to the base of the steps then back. Watching her, Kiernan caught the backdrop of frozen, horrified faces of the others. "Well, I'll tell you. I'm Felicity Robertson—not Roberts."

"Robertson?"

"Yes. My sister Hayley was murdered. We didn't know that, not for sure, not until last summer. But we did know she was gone. Disappeared. From her college campus. And Michael John Ralston was the last person to see her. Her boyfriend. The one who'd been part of our family, too, for three years. That's what we knew. That's what we had to deal with all these years. That's all we had to hold on to. Michael. The last one to see her."

"What the hell are you talking about? He wasn't. It all came out a year ago. His cousin murdered her and those other girls—*your* cousin. And you're talking about *Jack*? He was the one who was unjustly accused. The one who hadn't done anything, yet went through the hell not only of his girlfriend disappearing, but of nearly every last person he knew turning their backs to him. And you came here—as my *guest,* as *their* guest—as if *he* owes *you* an explanation? An apology? When I asked who you are, I wasn't by way of asking your name. I put those pieces together without you saying Robertson. I was asking what kind of person would think to do such a thing as this."

He heard Eleanor's soft, "Kiernan."

But he wasn't stopping now. "Not the woman I thought I—Not the woman I knew. Thought I knew."

"You don't understand. You have no…" Felicity shook her head, signifying the uselessness of words.

"I surely don't understand."

She paced again. Made a sound of impatience that her range was restricted. The steps on one end, Cahill the other. Him on one side, Ted, Ethan, and Paige seated on chairs on the other.

Thoughts and emotions flooded through his head, too many, too fast to be aware of any individual one.

So when he spoke, the words weren't the result of rational thought. "Did you know?"

She kept pacing.

"Did you know?" The repetition was a demand.

Elbows tucked in, she raised her open hands—a gesture of impatience and frustration. "Know? Know what?"

He held his tongue. Might have been one of the hardest things he'd ever done when he wanted to rail and rant at her. Wanted to simultaneously demand every answer from her and didn't want to hear a one.

She paced three more times, then said, still sharp, but somewhat quieter, "That Michael John Ralston now goes by the name Jack? Yes. I knew that."

The way she said that, concentrated and precise, he knew the answer, yet still had to ask: "When?"

She had her back to him, facing the steps. "Last summer. When it came out. About Ron, our cousin. All he'd ... done. But it didn't change the years that had gone before. They were still there. All that time, all those years. Knowing it was Michael. *Knowing* it. Knowing he got away with murder. And paid for nothing. For killing her. For ruining our family. For taking it all away. *He* did that. He did it all."

"He didn't."

She shot a look at him without making eye contact. "But he did. All of it. All except killing Hayley. The rest he did. We took him in to our family and loved him and he'd done that. So we closed off. No more taking anyone in. No loving anyone. Not only from the outside, but within ourselves. Protecting, always protecting against the possible pain. All the while, he's been here, living in his happy home, home on the range. And now he's walked away from me, just the way he walked away from Hayley. But he can't. I won't let him. He's not going to get away with it this time."

Cahill's grip on his arm stopped him when he instinctively moved toward her.

Kiernan strained against the hold for a moment, then stopped.

His brother was right. He had no way of getting through to her.

She'd made that clear with two words.

Last summer.

Two words that changed the meanings of so many things.

The barista who'd told him months after they met that Felicity had paid her to mix up their orders that first day. He'd dismissed it as jealousy.

Felicity's reluctance to meet his family. Not wanting to rush things, she'd said. Waiting for the perfect time.

Then a reserve, almost a caution when she finally did meet everyone but Jack and Valerie. Shyness, he'd thought.

She'd been hesitant about coming to the wedding, but hadn't that been so he'd persuade her, insist even? To make absolutely sure it happened.

She'd used him.

Every day. Every touch. Every moment together. Using him.

He'd been only a weapon for her to use against Jack and Val.

To come here. To hurt Jack. To disrupt their wedding.

From what seemed a great distance, he heard Eleanor suggest to someone that they take Felicity to the ranch office for now and say that she and Cahill would take him to the little house where they were staying.

What the hell difference did it make where he went now?

CHAPTER SIXTEEN

Val, his talkative, bubbling creek of never-ending words had said little.

She'd caught up with him, slipping her hand in his, then stayed beside him as he headed to a nonexistent destination. Where the past never caught up to you. Where its honed points never again pierced you.

He became aware of Val panting and slowed his pace, matching his strides to hers. But still they walked.

At least he knew where they were now. He adjusted their route, circling. Not back to the home ranch, but not straight away from it anymore, either.

Even now that he'd allowed her time to breathe, she said nothing.

Jack appreciated that. Almost as much as he appreciated her hand in his, her presence beside him.

He circled them back finally, coming up a gentle slope on the back of a rise. At its top, Val said, "Oh, now I know where we are."

From the top, they could see corrals, the barns and other outbuildings, then the compound of small houses clustered near the main house.

"What a beauty," Val said, looking down to the corral closest to them, one he used for newly arrived rescue horses. "That's a buckskin, right?"

"Yeah. And not such a beauty up close."

He felt her look. Knew it had to do with more than the horse.

Her one-word question confirmed it. "Scars?"

"Yep. And a temperament to match." His words also had to do with more than the horse. "Trick is to find out if that temperament's the cause or the effect of being mishandled."

"The effect. It's always the effect. Because no horse—no creature—deserves abuse. Anybody who tries to say it's the cause is too stupid to know how to deal with the situation."

He slanted her a look. "You don't believe anybody's born evil?"

"I don't rule out the possibility, but I haven't seen it. I believe most are born with the potential for evil. Then it depends on choices— theirs and other people's."

He grunted agreement. "That's true of horses. Mostly the choices of people."

"It's true of people, too," she insisted, "except with people the individual has responsibility. If they know the difference between right and wrong, they're responsible to not do wrong."

"You read about Hayley's cousin's upbringing."

"Yes. And the abuse from his step-father."

He gave one nod. They had talked about this a couple times since last summer. But it had been a lot more hypothetical, a lot more distant than it was now.

Lis had brought it all to the Slash-C. To Wyoming, where he'd come years before in hopes of leaving it behind.

"Nobody saw it," he said slowly. "I'm sure they didn't. Or they'd have done something. They wouldn't have closed their eyes to it."

"You mean Hayley's family. Nobody can know for sure what they saw or wondered or tried to ignore. Not even them. But even if they did see and ignored it, Hayley didn't deserve to be murdered."

"No, she didn't."

He wasn't sure where his mind went then. Not blank. He was sure of that. Yet, nowhere that he could trace back to when he became aware again, aware they'd been sitting there for a while in silence, Val up against his side, the warmth of her sustaining him.

They'd be married in a little over a day. She'd be his wife. He'd be her husband. And that was another kind of sustaining warmth.

"Hayley never called her Felicity, always Lis," he heard himself saying, "so I did, too. Her little sister Lis. Hayley said they were bookends, with the boys in the middle. There was a special bond there."

He felt Val's slight nod. "That's why she had such a crush on you."

"She didn't—"

"It's classic. Younger sister of an adored older sister either crushes on the boyfriend or hates him. She crushed on you."

"And now—"

"No. She might think she hates you, but she doesn't. That doesn't make her any less destructive."

They were silent as one cloud crossed over above them, then another.

He looked down and over to where Matty's army continued operating. All those people working to make their wedding a true celebration.

"I'm okay, Val," he said.

"No, you're not."

His mouth quirked. "I will be okay."

She looked at him a moment, then nodded. "Yes, you will."

The quirk became a grin. "I love you, Valerie Trimarco."

"I love you, Jack Ralston."

"I don't suppose you'd consider eloping with me right now."

"No. And neither would you. Not only would you lose your position as my mother's favorite and thus lose out on being the first called when she decides to cook up a banquet for the heck of it, but you also wouldn't get brownies. Not for a long, long time. Maybe ever."

He wanted to tell her again that he loved her. This woman who didn't say he was running away with his talk of eloping, who didn't cry out about all the wedding plans. This woman who knew he didn't mean it, even as a part of him wished he did.

"You're right. The benefits of eloping aren't worth running that risk—dropping down your mom's pecking order or the brownie ban. Okay, so the wedding's still on for tomorrow."

"Yup."

"I need to check Devil's water, see how he's settling in there. Want me to walk you back first?"

"No. But—"

"I know. The rehearsal's coming up and then the dinner. I'll get a shower, change, and be there on time. Don't worry."

"I'm not. What I started to say was but is Devil really what they named that poor horse?" At his nod, she added. "I'd liked to get my hands on that owner. Okay, he needs a name change."

"Some people think it's bad luck to change a horse's name."

"He's already had bad luck. He needs a change."

He stood, reached a hand down to her and gently helped her up. "Hope we didn't give little Gonzo too much jostling with the walk."

"Exercise is good for him. Just wish he could do it without me. Oh. I have it—the new name for the horse. Devil-May-Care—because we *do* care—and we'll call him DMC."

Donna, Irene, and Lucy had their heads together when Val and El came out of the room where Val had dressed for the wedding rehearsal and the rehearsal dinner.

As already arranged, Jack was getting ready at the main house.

The time walking and sitting with Jack had seemed real and important. All the plans and preparation for the wedding seemed distant and surreal.

Why hadn't she taken Jack more seriously? Why not cancel the whole thing and elope after all?

"No," El had said when Val spoke those words aloud.

El had been with Kiernan—*poor Kiernan*—but left him with Cahill to come help Val prepare for the rehearsal. All part of the Master Schedule that seemed unimportant right now.

"Because you and Jack would regret it later. You both deserve to have this wedding. To know how much you are loved. Both of you."

After that, El had been blessedly silent.

Perhaps knowing she'd won her point.

Jack not only deserved it, he needed it. He needed to experience people gathering to celebrate him and he needed to accept the outpouring of affection.

Val knew better than to hope for silence from her mother, and she had a feeling Donna and Irene wouldn't hold back, either.

But it was her father, with Ed behind him, who came up to her. Jimmy Trimarco took her hand. "Tell me what you want, Baby Daughter."

She knew exactly what he meant.

"Jack is strong enough, but I'm not sure I am. I don't want her here. There's probably nothing to do tonight, but tomorrow…"

"Consider it done." Her father kissed her cheek. "Let's go practice this wedding ceremony so my knees don't shake so badly tomorrow I can't get you down the aisle."

The rehearsal was exactly what they all needed.

It went completely and totally wrong.

There were trips, flubs, knots, spills, stutters, drops. Cahill played a bad chord, said a word that everyone knew had to be a curse, but since it was in Gaelic no one but Eleanor knew what it meant. At one point, even the minister, who'd done the service many times, went totally blank about what came next.

The only choice was to cry or laugh.

They laughed.

And laughed again. And laughed harder.

Until a few tears leaked out, taking with them, the first, sharp sting of the pain.

"… and then, if we've all survived to this point," Rev. Foley said, "I'll tell you that you may kiss your bride."

Jack jumped the gun by kissing her right then.

Another antidote to pain … not only theirs, but that of those watching them, those who loved them.

The rehearsal dinner was as relaxed as the red-checked napkins, corn on the cob, ribs, potato salad, and melt-in-your-mouth rolls.

The mood was also relaxed, though somewhat subdued.

Everyone at this dinner had also been there at lunch. Tomorrow, with the broader population of guests arriving, there'd be plenty of people unaware of what had happened. But not tonight.

They all knew what had happened.

They all recognized the absence of Felicity and Kiernan.

They all supported Jack and Val.

Earlier, Paige, Hannah, and Mandy had escorted Felicity to the ranch office. They'd found her tissues, drinking water, headache pills.

But she hadn't been crying, barely drank, and didn't take a pill. She also said very little.

After a few exchanged looks, Hannah had sent Mandy off to help with the dinner preparations.

Eventually, Hannah had gently said to Felicity that one or both of them would stay with her if she wanted, but otherwise, they were going to get ready for the rehearsal dinner.

Felicity didn't look up. "Go."

When she'd finished her meal, Paige quietly approached Donna and Matty and volunteered to take Felicity a dinner tray. She'd seen Eleanor take a tray to the house where Kiernan was, but she suspected no one else had volunteered for this duty.

Donna gave her a hug, Matty got the tray ready.

Ethan appeared at her side and carried it to the office door, but they'd agreed Paige should go in alone.

After a monotone "Come in" answered her knock, Paige took the tray from him while he opened the door for her, then closed it behind her.

"I brought you dinner."

Felicity sat on the floor with her back against a couch, staring at the opposite wall.

"Thank you."

"You're welcome. I'll set it here on the desk."

Without looking up and still in the same monotone, she asked, "How was the rehearsal?"

Paige hesitated a moment, then slowly sat on the couch. If Felicity wanted to talk, maybe listening could somehow help this whole, awful situation. "I hear there was a lot of laughter."

Felicity's head dropped slightly, as if a weight had been added to the top of her head. "It should have been Hayley's wedding rehearsal. It should have been her."

"Hayley should have had a rehearsal and a wedding. She was cheated out of that. But not by Jack. And this was never hers. This is Val and Jack's. They will not be cheated out of theirs."

"I suppose everyone hates me."

"Do you care?"

Felicity's head came up, her eyes snapped, and her mouth opened. Then all that was gone.

"You don't understand."

That's what she'd said to Kiernan. "No, I don't."

"I thought you might, since you're an outsider, too."

Paige thought of how the Chalmers had taken her in to the heart of their family. She thought of how Val and Jack and all here at the Slash-C had taken the Chalmers and her in for this wedding celebration.

"No, I'm not. And if you are it's by your own choice. We've heard the whole story now and it seems to me you should be apologizing to Jack instead of—well, whatever it is you think you want to do to him. He never did anything wrong, yet he was treated as if he were responsible for your sister's disappearance. Not only was he treated like he was guilty when he was completely innocent, but he was shut off from grieving with anybody else."

"You don't understand."

Paige stood at the repetition of that phrase. Before she said something she shouldn't.

But at the door she turned back.

"I'll tell you something else I don't understand and that's your treating Kiernan this way. He does not deserve it. We—Ethan and I— saw you two together in the barn Thursday by accident and if there'd been any doubt before, it was clear that he's crazy about you."

She remembered that moment of wondering if she and Ethan had ever been *that* passionate. If they had ever had that sort of coming together as mutual adults.

And now, she could only remember what her mother said all the time about not knowing the whole story of anybody else's life or loves. You should never envy a slice of it, because there was so much you didn't know about the rest.

She was never going to be uninhibited.

Ethan was never going to be dashingly romantic.

They had a love that came from who they were, from who they'd become over the years as a couple.

Yes, they might be facing a major turning point and she had no idea where it would lead them. But she would never hurt him the way this woman had hurt Kiernan ... and herself.

She needed to take that pregnancy test. She needed to do it soon. And she needed to talk to Ethan.

"I tried to break it off," Felicity said miserably. "I tried to stop seeing him. I wouldn't have come here if he hadn't insisted."

Paige wasn't letting that pass.

"You went after him because of his connection to Jack. And even when you fell for him—don't bother to deny it, it's clear you return his feelings in spades—you didn't tell him the truth. As for putting the blame on him because he insisted you come to this wedding, that does not pass any kind of smell test. Give me a break."

Felicity had no answer.

Paige opened the door. "You've lost a lot today. For what? What did you possibly hope to gain?"

Paige's righteous indignation evaporated at the bottom of the ranch office porch steps.

Who was she to berate Felicity for keeping secrets?

She would never hurt Ethan the way Felicity had Kiernan. On the other hand, look at what she was keeping from Ethan.

Possibly keeping from him.

She turned toward their room and the waiting pregnancy test.

"How'd it go?"

Ethan.

There, waiting for her. Visible now that he'd stepped out of the gathering shadows.

He offered her his hand and she took it, as they walked back to the gathering.

Her hand felt warm and comfortable and safe in his as she related what had been said.

CHAPTER SEVENTEEN

"Val," Jack started once people had cleared their places and lined up for apple pie and ice cream for dessert.

"I know. There's a sliver of daylight left, so you're going back to that horse."

He knew the way she said it that they were good, that she was okay.

If their walk earlier and the kiss at the end of the rehearsal hadn't told him that, this did for sure.

"For a while. I'll be back before it's full dark." He'd hold her in his arms tonight, no matter what tradition said. Tonight and every night. "But first I can do some good there."

He read in her eyes that she thought it would do *him* good, though that wasn't what he'd meant. But he knew that's what mattered to her.

"Fine," she said, teasing, no strain in her voice, "you're right that's where you can do the most good. Just so you know, though, I absolutely will *not* accept a horse as a good excuse for missing the birth of Gonzo."

He moved in and kissed her deep, ignoring the hooting and hollering from their audience.

When they came up for air, he looked directly into her eyes and said so only she heard it, "I was there for Addie's birth. I'll be there for this birth just the same."

He saw the laughter in her eyes before he heard it in her voice. "Good heavens, I hope *not* just the same."

They laughed together, along with something deeper and richer, at the memory of his assisting as she gave birth to Addie in the back of her old station wagon that was stuck in a snow-clogged ditch. The two of them. And then the three of them.

"All right, go on." She gave him a nudge. "Go see to your horse."

This horse was different.

Most that Jack worked with had adopted the flight method ingrained in their breed and avoided human contact as much as possible. He understood that. He'd followed the same path.

With them he started by establishing a routine, then sitting quietly in the corral with them. Not challenging, not pushing.

This horse—Devil, or Devil-May-Care, or DMC—opted for fight more than other horses he'd seen. The horse's first response was to try to kick and/or bite.

Yeah, it was born of fear and it made sense considering the treatment that must have put those scars on the animal.

But understanding it didn't change a whole lot if you had a few thousand pounds of muscle and bone bent on making you go away. Fast.

As he had each time in the corral with this horse, Jack carried a coil of rope in case he needed to snap the end at DMC to redirect him into flight. So far he'd only used it with gentle, floating motions to guide DMC.

Now that Dax had moved DMC's paddock buddy to the next corral, then took up a position out of the range of this corral's lights, Jack was ready to work DMC some.

It required complete concentration on the horse under ordinary circumstances. With this horse it required even more.

No room to think of anything else. Past and present were gone. All that existed was this horse. The swish of his tail, the movement of his ears, the pace of his movements as Jack advanced toward him, unhurried, but relentless.

The moment hung in the balance. The animal shifted his weight, then arched his neck. *Damn, it was going to be fight.*

In the next instant, the horse spun away and trotted along the fence. Jack moved in, gesturing slightly and smoothly to keep him going. Around and around. Then getting ahead of him to turn him back the other way. Around and around and around.

DMC's pace slowed. His head dropped slightly to a more relaxed posture. But Jack wasn't letting up his focus.

That's probably why he didn't hear anything until the creak of the gate opening.

His first flash of thought was that it had to be a mistake. Everyone, including the guests, knew not to come near, much less in this corral.

There was no time for more than that flash.

"I want to talk to you," shouted a female voice from the direction of the gate, which hadn't creaked closed. "You think you can walk away and that's that? It's not. I won't let it be."

"Get out, Lis—"

It was too late.

Devil had pivoted and was charging, ears back, mouth open, directly toward where she stood, three yards into the corral.

He saw the instant she realized what was happening. Her fear. And her knowledge that she couldn't make it back to the gate in time.

As the horse passed where he was stationed in the middle of the corral, he threw himself toward the animal, hitting his rump, making him sidestep to keep his balance, while Jack fought not to go down himself.

He scrambled backward, staying between the horse and Lis, trying to keep his motions as unthreatening as he could while maintaining his space and not losing any speed. He started to slowly move backward.

"Stay behind me." He didn't look at her, didn't allow much volume. "Keep moving back as I do, but no separation between us."

"Okay," came a small voice.

He adjusted his route toward that voice without looking around.

The horse squared up to him, ears back. If he reared and kicked out, if Jack couldn't get out of the way of those double-barreled front hooves, he could get the wind knocked out of him at best or, worse, get something vital broken. Either way he wouldn't be much good to Lis.

"Michael," Lis said. He felt her hand on his back, letting him know he'd reached her.

The horse reared up, but the front legs didn't kick out. He came back down, went to one side, almost as if trying to get around Jack to get to Lis. Jack blocked him with an unhurried move.

Most often when a horse had trouble with one gender it was with men. Looked like this horse was different in another way.

"Jack," came a low, familiar voice. Dax Randall. "I'm at the gate."

"Okay." It was more than okay. If this horse kicked him or ran him down there was still somebody to get Lis out of here, and to keep the horse inside the corral.

He kept moving back slowly.

The horse—not living up to his new name of Devil-May-Care—reared again, but without advancing, then shook and bobbed his head.

It was a last hurrah, because then came Dax's soft, "Got her. Two feet back to the gate."

Those last feet were easy. So was closing the gate with the familiar creak.

Seeing her, with more resemblance to her sister showing than ever had before, wasn't easy.

The worry came out in harsh words, though still spoken in a low tone. "That was damned stupid. Everybody was told to stay away from here. And why. To open the gate and barge in like that? Do you know what could have happened? To you, to me, to that horse? And sure as hell the horse wouldn't have deserved it."

"I want—"

"I don't give a damn what you want. Dax, can you hand over that chair right past you?"

She sucked in a breath. "—to talk to you."

"No."

"You can deal with this horse later. Michael—"

He slowly put down the chair Dax had passed over to him. To keep from slamming it to the ground.

"I'm going to sit with this horse. To try to undo some of the damage you did to him—*more* damage than was already done to him. Through no fault of his. You are to get away from this corral and stay away from it."

"I'll see to it," Dax said, a hand on her arm.

"But—"

Jack turned his back to her and creaked open the gate, all his focus on the horse.

CHAPTER EIGHTEEN

SATURDAY

Before dawn, Paige sat in the bathroom alone, listening to Ethan's steady breathing.

She'd planned to stay awake last night, to do this after he'd fallen asleep.

But she'd been tired—especially after another round of line dancing practice, completed over Ethan's laughing protests—that Ethan had expressed concern again about her not bouncing back from the "food poisoning."

She'd held off agreeing to see a doctor, but acceded to his insistence that she have the bathroom first and uninterrupted so she could get to bed as soon as possible. She never heard him join her, though she'd dimly recognized snuggling against him.

Now, she slowly closed the bathroom door, turned the latch without making a sound, then drew the box out of the bag stuffed at the bottom of her purse.

The crackling of the plastic seemed explosively loud in the dim silence, but when she paused to listen again, there was no sound of stirring. Not of Ethan or anyone else.

She read the instructions twice, then set out the simple materials that promised to give an answer—not an absolutely definitive answer, she knew that. Still, an answer.

If it was yes, it would change everything. For her, for Ethan, for them.

If it was no, it might still change everything. Because of how she would feel about that answer.

And her uncertainly about how he would feel about either answer.

She drew in a slow breath, ignored the bit of shudder in it, and followed the directions carefully.

Val nodded to Bryan, who'd taken over sentry duty from Dax sometime during the night by sitting in the rocker outside the room where Felicity had been brought back to last night.

Kiernan, she knew, had slept on a couch in the living room in the main area, where El and Cahill and Sam were staying. He hadn't seen or spoken to Felicity since the scene at lunch.

El had told her that while trying to dissuade Val from coming here.

No chance of that.

Probably hadn't been from the moment Felicity had sprung her surprise on Jack yesterday.

Certainly hadn't been after Jack finally came to bed in the deepest dark and told her what had happened at the corral.

He had fallen asleep then.

She'd laid awake. Thinking. Preparing.

She heard movement inside the room. Had to be Felicity—Lis—Robertson.

She drew in one last deep breath, knocked sharply, then opened the door without waiting for permission.

Felicity didn't deserve privacy. She was here on sufferance.

The younger woman was folding a bright blue sweater into the suitcase open on the bed. She pulled it to her chest and froze.

Val advanced and said evenly, "You're booked on a flight today. Someone will drive you to the airport in plenty of time to catch it."

For an instant, Val thought Felicity would turn and run into the bathroom. She'd bet a lot that Felicity had thought she would, too.

Instead, the younger woman raised her chin and came forward. "Go ahead. Say it. You must be furious with me for ruining your wedding."

Before she spoke, Val took a moment to absorb the surprise of her own answer. "You haven't ruined anything. This wedding's about celebrating with the people we love and the people who love us, Jack and me. Turns out you aren't either."

Felicity flinched, but didn't retreat. "I suppose you want to demand to know what I thought I'd accomplish by coming here."

Val tipped her head, surprising herself again with her calm and clarity. "No. Even if I asked you, even if you told me what you think right now is the reason you came, I very much doubt it would be the truth. At least not the whole truth. You've got some growing up to do to truly know why you came."

Color came into Felicity's pale face. "Growing up to do? It's funny how having the older sister you idolized disappear can make you grow up fast. And then to watch your family crack and splinter from the unrelenting pain. Yeah, that makes you grow up fast. I see you agree."

"Oh, no, I wasn't nodding because I agree that you're grown up. I don't. Though I am deeply and sincerely sorry about what your sister, your family, and you went through. I was nodding because you confirmed my suspicion that you hadn't thought about anyone but yourself in coming here."

"I thought about my parents and my siblings. And I thought maybe I'd find some answers."

"That's bull." The snapped words surprised the younger woman. "Jack has no answers for you and you know it. The answers about what happened to your sister are held by your cousin who murdered her and those other girls—that's where you should go for what and how, though I doubt you'll ever get a satisfactory why, because there is no possible why that can satisfy anyone. It simply doesn't make sense that such a horrible thing should be done to Hayley or anyone else. The reason you came here is that you haven't yet found the courage to move forward. Not forgetting your sister, but not letting her death be yours, either. That's the message you should take back to your parents and siblings if they need it, and the lesson you need to learn yourself."

"You don't know anything about—"

"I know how Jack—Michael John Ralston—struggled after years and years and years of sorrow, loss, grief, and self-recrimination to take those steps back into life. Because *he* has that courage. But you didn't think about that when you came here. You didn't think about Jack and you didn't think about Kiernan."

A renewed flush surged up Felicity's throat and into her cheeks.

Val didn't relent. "Have you ever stopped to think of it from either of their points of view? Jack loved Hayley and he loved your family. He not only lost both, but your parents sued him for wrongful death—leaving no doubt that they believed he'd killed her. Do you have any idea what that did to him? Do you? And then it's discovered that she was actually killed by a member of your family. And has there been one word of apology to him? Regret? Gee, we were wrong?" She felt her temper rising and fought to hold it back. "No. Not a word in more than a year. Not until you showed up here under false pretenses and using Kiernan's love to—"

"I never meant to—"

"More bull. You did. You went after Kiernan. You reeled him in. You told him lies. All the while using him to find the perfect moment to launch your vitriol at Jack. Neither of those good men deserved to encounter you. I'll do my damnedest every day to make sure Jack's okay. But Kiernan… No one yet knows the harm you've done Kiernan." She flipped a hand. "Yourself as well. Yes, you've definitely done a number on yourself, too. But I don't particularly care about that. Jack and Kiernan, I do care about. And for them, the sooner you're gone, the better. So finish packing and fly back to where no one expects you to live a true life."

Val turned away, aware the younger woman was trying to come up with a reply. Not interested in hearing it.

Halfway to the door, she pivoted to face Felicity Robertson again.

"One more thing. Think about this: Hayley remains alive in the hearts of the people who knew and loved her. Each time one of those people seals up his or her heart, Hayley dies a little more. You might not care about Jack or Kiernan, but don't do that to your sister."

Donna Roberts emerged from the bathroom, where she'd been gathering toiletries to help speed the packing.

Felicity still stood, holding the sweater she'd been folding before Val entered the room.

"I believe I got all your things." Donna placed the kit beside the suitcase.

"Did you hear what she said to me?"

"Oh, yes. Val made herself quite clear."

Ethan woke with a jerk at the light knock on the door to their room.

The bathroom door was closed, so presumably Paige was up and getting dressed.

A glance at the clock told him it was later than he'd thought.

He pulled on jeans to answer the door.

It was Bryan, the young ranch hand.

"Sorry if I woke you. Donna asked me to get Paige. Kiernan's girl—Uh, Felicity asked if she could talk to her. She's kind of—" He sent Ethan a look seeking support. "—upset."

Inwardly, Ethan groaned.

But he knew Paige.

He also knew she wasn't going alone.

"We'll be right there."

"C'mon in," Jack invited. He'd opened their kitchen door in answer to a knock to find Ethan Chalmers there.

Val saw Ethan was backed by Donna. She tensed. Especially when the older woman patted Jack's arm as she passed him.

This wasn't going to be good.

Why couldn't they be left to have a quiet breakfast on their wedding day?

"Hi, E-tan. Hi, Mrs. Donna," Addie called out cheerfully from the table, having picked up Sarah's pronunciation of his name.

"Addie, honey," Val said, "why don't you go to the main house and find Brennan and Finn and the others. Mr. and Mrs. Moski should be here soon if they're not already, and they're going to have lots of fun games for you this morning, then a picnic lunch."

At the mention of Brennan, Addie had slid off the chair. "Before I'm the flower girl? Because I'm the flower girl today."

"That's right," Val said, tousling her hair. "But a little later."

"Okay." Instead of going straight out, though, the little girl stopped by Jack at the doorway, hugged him around the legs and said, "It'll be okay, because Daddy Jack's not scared anymore."

Then, apparently unaware she'd landed a blow that sucked air out of the adult lungs in the room and brought tears to her mother's eyes, Addison Rose Trimarco soon-to-be Ralston skipped out of the room and off to find her friends.

Val swallowed. "What's going on?"

She'd addressed Donna, but Ethan answered.

"Paige is with Felicity. She asked us—well, Paige—to come talk to her a couple hours ago. I guess because we were with her yesterday or… I don't know why."

"Because Paige is a good listener," Donna said quietly. "Without letting her—or anyone—off the hook."

Ethan shot Donna a look, like he wondered what that detour into not letting people off the hook was about, but said only, "She is a good listener, though Felicity hasn't said much. Not until… Uh, well, what it comes down to is, she—Felicity—asks if you'd be willing to talk with her."

He was looking at Jack, but Val immediately said, "No."

"Yes." Jack add a crooked grin to his contradiction, looking at her. "How's that for a change? You saying no to talking and me saying yes."

"Then I'm coming, too."

"No, you're not. Think of it from her standpoint."

"*Her* standpoint? She came here under false pretenses, springing it on you, and using Kiernan in the process and you want me to think of it from *her* standpoint?"

He kissed the top of her head. "I'm going."

She'd known it even before her initial *no*. But she wasn't done.

"Talk to her in the ranch office. Where you have all the authority."

He kissed her again. "Glad you're in my corner."

"Good idea," Donna said. "Nobody's staying in the office until tonight."

"Thanks, Donna. C'mon, Ethan. You bring her to the office and I'll be there in a minute."

"Because he's going to check on the horse first," Val told the room at large.

Jack half chuckled. "Donna, if you'd…" He tipped his head toward Val.

"I'll be right here with Val," she promised him.

The door closed behind the two men.

"This is wrong. He was okay last night, but this… No one should ask this of him, least of all her. He spent so long blaming himself—"

"But he doesn't blame himself now, Val. He's strong enough. He is." She pressed Val down to a chair and sat facing her. "He's a man who heals animals who have lost their trust, their hope. He knows most—especially the ones hurt real bad by their lives—can't heal themselves. Just like he couldn't do for himself. But you healed him."

"He—"

"Oh, I know he did a lot himself. But you closed the wound enough for the healing to start. He knows how lucky he is. He wants to pass it on. To help that girl if he can. At least a little."

CHAPTER NINETEEN

Jack stepped in to the ranch office.

Felicity had been pacing, but stopped at the sound of the door, and turned.

She and Hayley were both blends of their parents, but in different proportions, so there was a resemblance without a lot of similarity.

"You came. It was so long I thought you weren't coming." Her words were too flat to convey surprise or anything else.

"They said you want to talk with me."

"Don't you want to talk with me? Don't you want to know about us? What happened with us? How the years without Hayley affected us? Don't you care at all?"

He removed his cowboy hat and tapped it against his leg. "Is that really what you want to know? Or do you want to get it off your chest that you still blame me despite it being your cousin who murdered Hayley?"

She sucked in a breath. "God, you *don't* care. I was the one who held on the longest, you know, who kept saying it couldn't be you. That you wouldn't hurt her. And now—"

"And now you can't let go of believing I did. That I was the culprit. Hayley always said you were too stubborn for your own good."

"How dare you quote my sister—?"

"I'll tell you how I dare. I dare because I loved Hayley and she loved me. And that gives me the right to remember her and things she said. I dare because I finally made peace with the fact that I didn't save her. I dare because you and your family didn't believe not only in me, but in Hayley and me loving each other. I dare because after all these years of being alone, I love another woman and her daughter and by some miracle they love me, and you come to the celebration of that fact and make a scene. That's how I dare."

She'd started crying somewhere in the middle of that speech. He wasn't sure exactly when. Now she plopped down on the sofa she was in front of and cried in earnest.

"I didn't know if I could go through with it. Coming here. A thousand times I thought I wouldn't. Not just coming here, but all of it with Kiernan."

Jack went to the sturdy coffee table and sat in front of her. Not touching, but close enough to make it hard to look at anywhere other than each other.

He realized with a bit of a jolt that she must be at least three or four years older than Hayley had been when she disappeared. When she died. When she was murdered.

In some ways Felicity seemed a lot younger. In another way far, far, older. No innocence left. No trust in the world. No trust in herself.

"You used Kiernan to find me?"

She nodded.

"After the news broke last summer?"

"Not right away. Only after… It was a couple months, after the shock was past and then realizing that knowing wasn't going to mend things. I always thought—everyone always said that not knowing was the hardest. But knowing didn't heal us—me. The holes were different, but still there. The pain… I had to do something. *Something.* That's when I started researching, looking. I knew you were in Wyoming from the news reports, but nobody ever got to see you, to interview you. Maybe if I'd seen you… I had to know. I kept digging. It was one line in a report. It said you were rumored to be involved with a woman named Valerie from Gloucester. I spent two weeks there, digging and digging. But in the end it was luck—"

He noticed she didn't say if it was good luck or bad luck.

"—that I was having lunch in a little restaurant on the beach where people knew her and they were telling each other how you'd just arrived from Wyoming, telling her you loved her." A fresh spurt of tears came at that. Then, oddly, a faint smile that she didn't seem to be aware of. "It was Kiernan who came in with the news. I saw him and… But he didn't see me. I stayed in the corner and listened to everything. Then I went back and started planning. I moved to Boston. Found a job near where Kiernan worked. Arranged to meet him."

"And played him perfectly to make him interested in you by pulling back right at the points he'd usually be losing interest. So, instead of losing interest, he fell all the harder."

She looked directly at him. "It wasn't to make him fall harder. I… I wasn't sure I could go through with it. That's why I kept putting off meeting you last winter when he invited me to family gatherings in Gloucester."

"And was that why you didn't take him to see your family?"

She twisted her shoulders, part shrug, part flinch. "They aren't the way you remember them. Any of them. The boys… I suppose they're okay. But my parents… they're not the way you remember," she repeated.

"You don't know how I remember them."

For the first time a flicker of something other than misery showed in her face. Not strong enough to be called curiosity.

He spoke to that flicker. "The way I remember your parents best is when I saw them in the hallway of the police department when they came after I reported Hayley missing. Looking at me, asking me without asking if I'd hurt her, harmed her. If I was responsible. And then the last time. At the courthouse. After the judge ruled I wasn't guilty of wrongful death. But your parents still looked at me with their absolute certainty that I'd killed Hayley and that I was extending a portion of their torment by refusing to admit it. That I could give them that relief if I wanted to." He looked away from her. "There was a point I considered doing that. Seriously considered killing myself and leaving a note saying I was responsible. To end that part for everybody. Including me."

She made a sound.

He looked at her again. It had been a sob, letting out a fresh run of tears.

"It all just sucks," she said.

"It does." He handed her a tissue box from the coffee table. "You need to find a way to live, Felicity. To let go of being stuck in that time, that night—" He swallowed. "The night Hayley disappeared. The night she was taken from all of us. She'd be on your tail about that. You know she would. And even without that, you deserve to have a life. You need to find it."

"I don't know how."

"Yes, you do." She looked up at that. "I knew how, too. Didn't have the courage to do it. Not until Valerie Trimarco kicked my butt. With a little help from Addison Rose Trimarco."

That surprised her. "Addie? That little girl—?"

"Don't let her size fool you. She can pack a wallop. Just like her momma. She put her hands on my face and said *Don't be scared, Jack.*" He shook his head. "Four words from a tot. *Don't be scared, Jack.* It was my whole life right there. Keep on being scared or truly face what had happened and still have the courage to live. That's what you need to decide now, Lis—Felicity. Go on being scared or take a chance at living. Because I'll tell you something I realized last year—holding on to the anger and the pain, that's not holding on to Hayley. Neither was trying to feel nothing. They all diminish Hayley, who she was and how she lived. How she loved."

Tears flowed down her cheeks, dropped from the edge of her jaw, spread dark on the fabric of her shirt.

They sat there for a while.

He couldn't blame her if she wished they could sit there forever, but he couldn't. Wouldn't. He had a wedding to get ready for. A life— and love—to live.

"It's time, Lis. Time for me to get back to celebrating that Val and Addie love me. That I love them. That we're going to live. I truly hope you'll—"

"I'll leave right away. If you could arrange a ride to the airport. Maybe Bryan or…"

He stood. "We'll see to it that you get a ride, if that's what you want. I'll say good-bye. And good luck."

She looked up. "Good-bye, Jack." It was the first time she'd used the name that had moved him forward eventually.

He put his hat on and went to the door.

But there he stopped. Debating with himself.

On one side was many years of staying separate, even distant from other people. All other people, even the ones who'd cared for him.

On the other side was Val.

No big surprise which won.

"I've got one more thing to say to you, Lis." He waited until she met his eyes and this time he saw a faint light of curiosity in hers.

That could be a good start for her.

"All last winter, when Kiernan was inviting you to come to Gloucester and meet his family, you could have confronted me then. Nothing to stop you. Accept any one of his invitations, walk in and blast away at me the way you did here. You didn't do that. But you did start going to Gloucester and meeting the family as soon as Val and Addie and I came back here. You could have jumped at this chance, too, but what I hear is you were trying to *not* come, while Kiernan was pressuring you to be here. Now, somebody looking at that might come to the conclusion that you were dragging your feet because you didn't want to end what was going on with Kiernan."

"No. I was using him. All along. I was working up my nerve."

"I don't think so. Because here's the other thing. From that first day, sitting in The Fishwife in Gloucester, what was stopping you from marching up to Val's front door, pounding away and demanding to see me? Sure you might've had the door slammed in your face, but I was out and about a fair bit in those months. Walked the beach every day. You could have found me and told me what you wanted to say months and months ago. But, instead, you found a way to get introduced to Kiernan. To spend all these months together. Telling yourself all the while that you were after me, but being with Kiernan day in and day out. Getting closer and closer."

She stared at him. Maybe gaped.

He nodded, tugged on the brim of his hat and left.

Ethan watched Jack leave the ranch office and head back again toward the corral where he was working with that rescue horse.

Ethan had been occupying this spot ever since he and Paige had walked Felicity to the office.

Paige had stayed with Felicity for a few minutes. When she came out, she'd spotted him here, leaning against the corral fence where he could see the comings and goings. Not intruding, but close enough to be on hand if his help was needed.

"Some fun, huh?" he'd asked as Paige came up to him.

"Sometimes emotions get messy. Sometimes life does, too."

She sounded a little strange. Calm, like she always—usually—was, but with something underneath.

"Are you feeling okay?" he asked.

"Yes. Looks like there are lots of people on hand to help, so I'm going to go in and get ready for the wedding. That way I'll be available to help while everyone else is getting ready."

He pushed off the fence.

Her hand on his shoulder nudged him back. "Why don't you stay here, in case they need anything? We'll get ready faster if we do it separately."

He watched her all the way to the door and inside.

Then he forced himself to turn away. What was going on with her? Something was definitely … different. Different and *off*.

He wasn't stupid.

He knew he should be wondering if her feelings for him had changed. Maybe his head *was* wondering it.

But his heart, his bones, his … *soul* didn't buy it. Because if Paige no longer loved him, the universe would crumble. Yet here it sat with the sun up, the clouds zipping across the sky, the earth solid beneath his feet.

Behind him, a door opened and closed.

Before he turned, he knew it was Mandy.

She came up beside him, mimicking his posture leaning against the fence.

"Hannah said Felicity asked for you and Paige."

"Yeah."

"Fun," she said dryly.

It struck him she'd used the same word, the same intonation he had. They used to do that all the time when they were younger.

"Nope. She wanted to talk to Jack."

She groaned.

"He agreed. Just left her a bit ago."

"So you're waiting here to see if somebody needs to pick up the pieces."

He didn't need to confirm that. "Giving them the option of somebody not directly involved."

"Mmm."

The sound couldn't have been any more neutral. Yet he knew she approved. He also knew her mind traveled away from that as they stood there in silence.

"What's wrong with Paige?" Mandy asked abruptly.

His twin radar had told him that was coming before she spoke. "That food poisoning hit her harder than we knew."

She gave him the side-eye.

Not only did she not buy that, but she thought he was an idiot for buying it himself.

Did he buy it?

Maybe not, considering he hadn't insisted in the face of Mandy's side-eye.

Paige certainly had been sick. And what else could it be other than the food poisoning? Unless it was a stomach bug affecting her differently from any he'd known her to have before.

The sudden aversion to the sachet she loved so much that he put up with it being in his suitcase, too, the naps, the short temper—by her standards, anyway. The secretiveness, distance.

Secretive and distant? Paige?

Whoa. Where had that thought come from?

Was she being secretive? Distant?

Mandy spoke abruptly. "It was my fault."

"What?"

"It was my fault they crashed."

His twin radar was at a loss, presumably having been distracted by his internal questions about Paige. "Who crashed?"

"*Who crashed?* Who do you *think* crashed? Mom and Dad, of course."

"How was it your fault when you were at home in North Carolina—well, at the high school by the time the plane went down? Anyway, they were a state away in Georgia."

"Because we had that horrible fight that morning—*I* had that horrible fight with them. About going to that stupid dance and I was so mad they were letting you go with Paige and they said no to me going—"

"With a guy three years older with a lousy reputation. Not the same as my going with Paige at all."

"Of course, because you were always the perfect, responsible one and I was the wild child who made Mom cry and Dad get angry that morning because I said horrible, horrible things, then stomped out and never said—" She sucked in a breath. "And then they left, still upset because of what I'd said, what I'd threatened, and—"

"They crashed hours later. I can't imagine anyone was still crying after all that time. Besides, Dad was piloting and—"

"Do not make it all reasonable and logical. It was my fault. *My* fault. I was a selfish brat and they *died*. Oh, my God, they died. So horribly, so—"

He wrapped his arms around her and closed them into a bear hug. "It wasn't your fault. It wasn't my fault. It wasn't their fault. It wasn't Hannah's fault. It was a damned awful thing to happen, and it wasn't our fault."

"Then why have you been trying to make up for it ever since?"

"What?"

She pushed back to look up at him, dashing her tears away with jerky motions, like she was angry at them. "You can kid a lot of people, but you can't kid me, Ethan. I know—I knew from the beginning that you blamed yourself. You thought if they hadn't delayed to drive you to early football practice that day that they would have landed earlier and—"

"It would have been the same amount of flying time. It wasn't the time they took off. It was the amount of flying time."

"See, you have been thinking about it. You've thought it was your fault and that's why you go all uptight and taking care of everything and planning every last detail down to the second and—" She waved a hand. "And all that. As if having the right plan would keep anything bad from ever happening again. And all the time it was my fault."

He frowned deeply at her. "That's what you've thought all these years?"

"Of course it is. I got them all upset and—"

"No, you didn't. They were fine when they dropped me off at practice. Besides, in the report, the people at the airport said they were joking. One said the last he saw of them was Dad with his arm around Mom as they walked to the plane, and he could hear them laughing."

She blinked up at him. "You read the report on the crash?"

"Of course. I wanted the facts."

"When?"

"As soon as it was available."

"You never told me that."

"You never wanted to talk about it. Any of it." He frowned. "You've never talked about that day at all." Until now.

"No. I didn't. Not after… I tried once and you got even more uptight and taking care of the entire world than ever. So I stopped. I didn't want to make it worse. I didn't want you getting even deeper into taking on all the responsibility for it when I knew—When I was sure it was mine."

"You want to read the report? I can forward you the file."

She almost chuckled. "That is so you, Ethan. Make it all better with a scientific report."

"It's the facts."

"I… No. I don't want to read it. Not yet." Her mouth twisted. "Maybe eventually. But what I said before about you trying to make up for things still holds. Don't glare at me. It's true."

"I'm not trying to make up for anything—"

"Then why do you keep yourself and Paige and everybody else on a schedule as if one small change will let everything fall apart, as if they wouldn't have crashed if they hadn't deviated from their schedule that morning?"

"I don't—"

"You do, Ethan." She looked up at him, not letting him look away. "You do. And it's hurting Paige."

"Hurting her? That's the last thing—"

He stopped, but Mandy was giving him that look that always had a way of bringing him smash up against the immovable wall of truth. It made no difference if hurting Paige was the last thing he wanted. Not if he was, in fact, hurting her.

He was grateful for the distraction when a ranch truck stopped by the office. Donna Currick got out and went in with a suitcase.

So he was off Looking-After-Felicity duty. He could wrap up this conversation and go to their room to see Paige. He'd walk in and she'd be her usual self. Everything would be back to normal. It had to be.

Except Mandy was not distracted.

She expelled a long, slow "Ahhhh," which made him feel like a specimen under a microscope she'd just identified. "It's not to make up. It's to protect."

"It's common sense to—"

"To try to make everything safe for everyone else, but especially Paige. You always had an extra dose of that in you and after Mom and Dad it was like—Of course, of course, of course. Don't you see?"

"You're off on another of your tangents, Mandy."

"Don't you see what you've been doing?"

"What I'm doing is applying common sen—"

"No, no, no. You're trying to make sure nobody gets caught in the kind of bind Hannah was in trying to finish raising us. Like I said the other day, the scrimping and saving. And you said it, said it right out about making sure nobody has to go through that or any other kind of bind. But—"

"It only makes sense." First Hannah and now Mandy? What was going on?

"—it isn't always about sense," she finished triumphantly, having talked over him. "That's what I was saying about Paige. You're *drowning* her in good sense. You gotta give her something more."

"If she were the type of woman who craved drama, she wouldn't have fallen in love with me."

"Boy, is that the truth. Drama, or romance, or spontaneity or—"

"All right. I know your opinion, but she's a—"

"She's still a woman."

"—sensible person."

"You know, it's not even a woman thing." She was paying no attention to what he said. So at least *one* thing was normal. Though he still felt as if the ground under his feet had turned to marsh—No, no, that couldn't be true. It was solid. Still solid. Because the universe hadn't changed. Paige loved him. Everything was in order. Sane. "Even men like you who pretend they don't have a heart—"

"I never—"

She waved that off. "I know you do. Paige knows you do—bless her for the sweet, patient, saintly woman that she is to be in love with you."

"Hey."

"But the fact remains that everybody needs more than common sense, Ethan. They need to know that their needs, sometimes even their wants, come before a schedule. Doesn't all this—" She waved a hand toward Lisa putting final touches on the flowers at the altar, Dave directing placement of the hay bales while Taylor and two of Val's sisters-in-law spread quilts. Under the covering over the patio, Dax, Shane, and Val's brothers set up tables and chairs. Matty and Hannah followed, spreading tablecloths. "—give you ideas? Don't you see? All the other stuff happening, even all the pain Felicity's feeling and bringing that back up for Jack, none of that can defeat this— friends and family coming together to celebrate with Jack and Val. To celebrate the most important thing."

"Not until—"

"Forget your schedule for a minute and *feel*, Ethan. You've been so busy guarding against the bad stuff you're not letting yourself feel the good stuff." She pushed away from the corral fence. "I'm going to go help Matty and Hannah. But I hope you'll turn off your head long enough to listen to what's truly in your heart. Because if you do, I think we'll be having a wedding a lot sooner than your stupid schedule says."

CHAPTER TWENTY

Kiernan knocked on the front door of Donna and Ed's house.

He didn't know how El had discovered that's where Jack and Val were now, but he was grateful for the information.

He wasn't quite as grateful for the company.

Eleanor and Cahill had insisted on coming with him, though that had happened only after trying to persuade him that he shouldn't leave before the wedding.

The one thing they'd all agreed on was that he needed to talk to Jack and Val.

Before he left the Slash-C, he'd added.

Before you decide to stay, they'd countered.

So here he was, being told to "C'mon in" by Ed Currick's voice. And there were Val and Jack with him.

As soon as the older man saw who it was, he clapped his hat on his head, said a few words about needing to see to something, then headed out, resting a hand on Kiernan's shoulder as he went by.

"Jack, Val, I can't apologize enough for my role in—"

"What role?" Jack interrupted. "You didn't do anything but bring a guest to the wedding like we wanted you to."

"I appreciate your seeing it that way. But the fact remains I'm responsible for bringing her and that caused all this—" He muttered a phrase in Gaelic his mother would not approve of. "To bring that sorrow here to you at a time that should be only happy. So I'm saying here how deeply sorry I am, and then I'll be going, and—"

"No," Val said. Then she clamped her mouth closed and determinedly did not look at anyone else in the room.

Jack grinned slightly. "You heard the lady."

"But Jack," Val started. "He has a point—"

"He doesn't. It's none of Kiernan's doing."

"I brought her here," he repeated doggedly.

"Without knowing a thing," El said from behind him.

"We know *that*," Val said. "You can't have thought that we thought that you were part of—No, that has nothing to do with—"

"To do with anything." Jack had taken over her words and turned them the direction he wanted. "As I said to Felicity a bit ago, this is our celebration of me loving Val and Addie." His arm around Val tightened. "And them loving me. We want those happiest for us around us and that includes you, Kiernan."

"But—"

"Val wants you at her wedding. Don't you?"

Jack leaned over to look at her. She looked at her husband-to-be, then at Kiernan. "I do." Tears came into her eyes. "I want you at my wedding, at our wedding. Please stay."

From behind him, Cahill cleared his throat. Kiernan knew his older brother well enough to know that if he turned around he'd see tears in the man's eyes.

"You said you'd back me up on songs," Cahill reminded him.

"You can't say no now, Kiernan." El's soft words sealed the issue and they all knew it.

Kiernan was trying to come up with words to express that and everything else he felt when Jack saved him.

"There is one thing you could do for us, though," the bridegroom said.

"Of course. Anything—"

"Take Felicity to the airport."

"Jack," Val half gasped.

That about expressed how Kiernan felt about it, too, though he didn't make a sound. Or a move.

"Ed got her a flight. She needs to leave in about ten minutes to catch it. Go find Bryan and he'll fix you up with a ranch truck. Then swing by and pick her up at the ranch office. Donna's with her there now. You should make the round trip in good time to be back here for the wedding."

They didn't touch.

They didn't talk.

As far as Kiernan knew, they didn't look at each other.

Not in the whole drive to the airport. Not in his pulling her suitcase out of the back of the truck and rolling it in to the small building.

"Perfect timing," the cheerful woman behind the desk said. "They'll be boarding shortly."

"You don't need to wait," Felicity said when the woman behind the desk was done with her.

He said nothing. He waited.

It wasn't long. Not by the showing on the wall clock, anyway.

When the woman called to start boarding, it turned out they'd happened to stand where the line started.

She stepped away from him, toward the security entry. Then she stopped and turned.

"Kiernan, I'm sorry. I never meant—I never meant to hurt you."

She stretched up and kissed him on the cheek.

He didn't speak.

Didn't move.

Not until she'd passed through security and he felt the pressure of the other passengers behind him, too polite to tell him to move the big lump he'd become, did he shift to one side. He could still see her at the head of the line of passengers climbing the stairs into the small plane.

He felt the faint imprint of her lips on his skin fading, just as the momentary impression of her light scent did.

She never looked back.

And then the plane was gone.

"I don't like the look of those clouds."

Val had slipped out the back door when she was supposed to be in her bedroom, primping. But, really, it wouldn't take that long to get ready.

"Don't worry, Val," one of the ranch hands said to her.

"We've got it covered," added another.

Bryan nodded. "We're checking radar every five minutes. We have the drill for moving the bales into the barn and turning around the altar to under ten minutes. We won't let you get rained on during your wedding."

She looked around at the grinning faces and felt tears well in her eyes.

"Val?" Bryan looked worried.

"It's okay. In fact, it's wonderful. You all are wonderful. Thank you. Thank you all so much."

"*Valerie*," came Lucy Trimarco's voice from the house.

"Busted," Bryan said with a wink.

She chuckled. "You've got that right."

She started toward where her mother held the back door open, then turned back to Bryan and the others, hugging each one quickly.

Then she hurried back into the house.

It was almost time to put on her beautiful wedding dress.

"All set," Ethan said, coming out of the bathroom. He looked at her floral sundress. "You look great."

"Thank you." She met him in the space between the bed and bathroom, reaching up to undo one more button on his shirt.

He grinned. "I forgot. Casual."

"We have a little time and… Why don't you sit down?" She nudged him toward the easy chair, but he didn't sit. She pulled in a breath and said it. "I took a pregnancy test this morning, Ethan. It came out positive."

He looked blank. "Why would you—? Positive? What does that mean?"

"It means that if everything goes right we're going to have a baby."

He sat.

Fast.

"Now? Have a baby now?"

Caught between laughter and tears, she said, "Not right this minute, no. In eight months or so."

"But we were going to try two years after we bought a house and we allowed five years after that in case…"

"Yes." She sat on the edge of the bed across from him. "In case I couldn't conceive."

"We have to work another two years before we get married, and then the next step is saving the amount we need for a down payment—"

"The amount you want to put down. Not need."

"—on a house. That all comes before we try to have a baby. This is all wrong." The words came out as if unattached to the whirl of fragmented thoughts and shock she could see flooding him.

Paige felt herself contract inside.

She wasn't angry at him. She wasn't even sad. She wasn't anything.

"Okay, Ethan."

"How could you be pregnant? All the doctors said it would be nearly impossible for us to get pregnant without treatment. That's why I factored in saving for those expenses for after we're into our house."

"Look at the bright side. We wouldn't have to spend that money."

"Why would you even take a pregnancy test? Where did you get it?"

She knew it was his way of coping—focusing on the practicalities. "I got it when I went into town yesterday morning because I've had some symptoms."

She thought about telling him what Hannah had said, but decided not to draw in his sister. This was for the two of them to work out.

"What symptoms?"

She told him.

"But all those are subjective." He sounded a bit more like himself.

"They are. But they're subjective about *my* body, which I know pretty well. And there's the darkened areolas."

"I didn't notice."

"You were otherwise occupied."

His gaze went to the bodice of her dress. "You could—"

"I'm not going to show you now, Ethan. Besides, there's the positive test result."

He frowned. His trying-to-make-sense-of-something-that-made-no-sense frown. "What did you mean we wouldn't have to spend that money?"

"Because we conceived this baby without the expensive treatments." She tried a small smile. "We're actually saving money."

"But... But... This isn't the right time. We're not even married yet."

"No, we're not. And we don't have the money in the bank that you want. Or the security of a house bought with a huge down payment. We don't have any of that. And I know how much it means to you, Ethan. I know how much you need that. I also know that I've sprung this on you, while I've at least had the time while I suspected to grapple with the possibility."

"You've suspected? How long? Why? Why didn't you tell me?"

"Because I didn't want you to have to face this if it wasn't true."

He blinked at her. "But are you sure?"

"The test can show a false positive, and a doctor would be the true confirmation, but... I'm sure."

"A doctor. We'll get you to a doctor. It might be that food poisoning still affecting you."

"It's not." She stood. "We'll talk about this later. But I will tell you one thing now. I love you. I have always loved you. I always will love you. And I know how this disrupts all the plans and certainty you need, what an adjustment for you that will be. But I am keeping this baby, whether it's with you or without you. I heard what all those doctors said, too. The treatments aren't a guarantee. This might be my one and only opportunity. I'm having your baby, Ethan Chalmers, and I refuse to be anything but ecstatic about it."

She didn't sound ecstatic. She sounded determined. But at least she didn't feel constricted inside anymore.

And, separate from how Ethan reacted or felt, there was this solid, sure core inside her that felt right, so very, very right. That was a start toward ecstatic.

She'd reached the door before she turned back to him, still sitting in the chair.

"C'mon, or we'll be late for the wedding."

The weather cooperated.

They were done fussing with her and now El and Matty were making their final preparations while Donna and Lucy kept Addie and Brennan in their present pristine state.

The hay bales were arranged around the entrance to the barn, like a maze made for wandering, with plenty of good views to the front, just the way she'd asked. Each was covered with gaily colored quilts.

As a backdrop to the altar, the barn doors were left wide open, with fabric loosely draped at either side and held back with flowers. Then more flowers flanked the doors in the huge pots that were at peak bloom.

The open doors framed where Jack and the others stood, with the darkness behind them of the barn's dim interior highlighting the cloth-draped altar, the minister, Dave, Cal. And, especially, Jack.

Jack, Dave, and Cal wore sharp, pressed jeans with dress shirts so white they dazzled, pale gray vests, cowboy hats, and black boots.

"What are you doing, Valerie?" Donna asked as she passed the open door to the bathroom and found the bride with a corner of the curtain held aside.

She grinned. "It's bad luck for the groom to see the bride, but nobody ever said anything about the bride peeking at the groom."

"What do you think of what you see?"

She turned and beamed at the other woman. "Gorgeous. Absolutely gorgeous."

Donna chuckled. "The man or the setup."

"Both. And thank you for all you've done for both." She hugged the older woman.

"Ready!" Matty called from the front room.

It was time.

CHAPTER TWENTY-ONE

If Kiernan had hoped his return from the airport would keep him from being there for the wedding, he was disappointed.

He hadn't wanted to hear the pledging of love and life.

…or maybe he had.

Because he'd pushed the speedometer on the truck higher and higher … until here he was, walking among the other guests, the women's bright dresses like a field of summer flowers, all the happy voices calling out greetings as they filled in the hay bale pews.

But it wasn't the voices that cut through Kiernan's numbness.

It was the sound of Cahill's guitar. Soft melodies seamlessly blended the traditional songs of his childhood, western tunes, and sections of familiar ballads made special by Cahill's love affair with his guitar.

One of Kiernan's earliest memories was lying in his small bed, supposedly asleep, but listening to his older brother play. Cahill's guitar was the soundtrack of his life—losses, triumphs, celebrations.

Somehow it seemed preordained that he'd be hearing that music at this moment.

It also seemed like the fates were doing their damnedest to rub it in what a fool he'd been.

At least with Cahill playing for the ceremony, Eleanor the matron of honor, and their son sitting with the Trimarcos, Kiernan was free to take a seat alone and well toward the back.

That didn't last.

Hannah Randall came by, hooked a hand in his arm and tugged. "You're going to come sit with us and—"

"Thanks, but—"

"—I want to have a good view of Dax, so we're sitting close to the front. Besides I promised Eleanor I'd make sure you were with us."

He sighed, got up and followed her. Paige and Ethan were at the other end of the row, then Mandy, Sarah, Chalmers, Hannah, and he sat on this end.

That turned out to be a mistake. It meant he was accessible to the Trimarco clan as they came in and found seats. He got pounded on the back or cuffed on the arm by the males and patted on the cheek or shoulder by the females.

He wanted to stand up and walk out. Better yet, run. And keep running for a long, punishing time. Only he couldn't do that to Val and Jack. Or to Cahill and El. Or the Randall/Chalmers family. Or the Trimarcos and Curricks.

All he could do was sit here and take it—their concern, their support.

He shifted, catching a glance of Paige and Ethan in intense conversation.

He wanted what they had.

The knowledge hit him harder than any of the Trimarcos had.

He never had wanted that before.

Even watching Cahill and El start their family, knowing how happy they were, still he'd been positive he wasn't ready for that. Wondered in the back of his head if he'd ever be.

Cahill was the steady, solid McCrea brother. He'd occupied the territory at either extreme. More of a partier, more of a recluse at times.

But now...

Now he knew that he wanted it—what Paige and Ethan had, Cahill and El, Dax and Hannah, all this Currick clan and their friends, the Trimarco clan. And now Val and Jack.

Now he knew. Now that the woman he'd wanted it with was gone.

Gone in a way far deeper than an airplane heading away from him.

Because this going took away their past, along with their future.

All in a moment of betrayal.

Hello, Michael. Sorry, I can't call you Jack.

And then Cahill began to play and sing. A song about finding The

One.

His own brother.

Not fair.

Not fair a't'all.

"Is this thing ever going to start?" Jack grumbled under his breath to his best man as they stood by the altar.

Dave chuckled. "Waited till the last minute for your first sign of cold feet, didn't you?"

"No cold feet. I want to be married to Val. Now."

"Shouldn't be much longer. This song Cahill's starting? It's the one for the kids and Matty and Eleanor to come down the aisle and do you know what it's called?"

Jack felt a tug at his mouth. "I do. 'Haste to the Wedding.' "

Dave chuckled. "That should make you feel better."

"There's stirring in the house," Dax whispered.

"*That* makes me feel better."

Brennan, dressed in miniature duplicate of the three men standing here at the front of the gathering, carried what looked like a sign made from wood as he made his way toward the front. But Jack couldn't see the sign with all the people between them.

Brennan started off okay but then was sidetracked, walking down one of the side aisles and talking to people. There were a lot of chuckles as helpful guests steered him back on his way to the front.

The sign was now tipped back over his shoulder. He started down another side aisle, but Dave gave a whistle, and pointed where he was supposed to go. Brennan flapped his free hand against his side to indicate the craziness of all this, but returned to the main path.

Finally Jack could see the sign and understand the growing chuckles. The sign said: "She's coming soon, Jack."

As Brennan broke free from the hay bales, he spotted his grandfather, waved, and continued jauntily to his father.

Addie, with a full sense of drama, waited for all eyes to come to her at the back. She wore cowboy boots and hat—matches for Brennan's—a denim top and a pink tutu skirt.

Jack had a feeling she'd been her own stylist. He grinned as she started negotiating her way down the zigzag aisle with aplomb.

She, too, carried a sign, though hers had no handle, so she held it between her hands, turning this way and that to show the guests.

Hers said, "From now on, I'm calling him Daddy."

Jack swallowed, swallowed again, then gave it up. He held out a hand and Addie went to him. As he pressed her to his side, he pressed at his eyes with thumb and index finger of the other hand.

How the heck was he going to get through this?

When he looked up again, Lucy and Donna had taken seats up at the front.

Matty, then Eleanor, came along that erratic aisle that only Val could have designed, in dresses that sure looked like the same color to him, even if one called it seafoam and the other misty sage.

They gave him a break, since they only smiled broadly at him, presenting no risk to his tear ducts.

And then it was Val.

He supposed her father was there, because he was supposed to be, and he doubted Donna and Lucy would have let anything else happen than what was supposed to. But he didn't see him.

He saw only Val.

His Val.

The minister was saying the words that were marrying Jack and Val.

Ethan heard them.

But the words he heard better were Paige's.

I didn't want you to have to face this if it wasn't true.

But *she* had faced it. Before she knew if it was true and after. Grappled with it. Wondered. Probably worried.

Alone.

That wasn't how it was supposed to be.

That wasn't how *they* were supposed to be.

"Why didn't you tell me?"

"Shh. I told you."

"Not right away."

"No. Now shhh."

"You wanted to wait until you were sure?"

"Uh-huh."

"But until a doctor—"

"I'm sure."

He sat back a moment, then leaned in again. "But you were dealing with it alone before you were sure."

She turned her head. He'd come in so close in order to whisper that the movement swung her hair across his nose. He wanted to bury his face in it.

"I couldn't avoid dealing with it. It's … there." Her hand had started toward her belly, but stopped.

"Were you scared? *Are* you scared?"

She looked into his eyes. "Yes."

He looked at her, this woman he loved with everything there was in him. "Me, too."

He sat back and tried to listen to the ongoing ceremony.

"Some people make a braid from three strands to represent the unity they are entering into. Valerie and Jack had another idea," Reverend Foley told the audience with a smile. "Ed, I understand you're going to tell us about what they're doing?"

As he spoke, benches were brought out and set a good distance apart. Each had a round metal piece set vertically like an old-fashioned coffee grinder, complete with crank handle.

"This is an old cowboy rope-making machine that was in my mother's family as long as she could remember," Ed said. "It was used to make the rope for her family's ranch in the early days.

"We're honored to have it put to use again, and in this way. Jack and Val and Addie are going to use it to make a wedding rope, showing how they've come together. Jack's going to sit at one end and Val at the other end. Addie, you're going to be here with me in the middle, because you're going to have the real important job of keeping the knots out. But first, we need to thread the strands. Val, only seems right that you get to do the first strand."

She took the strand Ed held out, hooked it at the end she'd be occupying, walked it to the machine Jack would use, hooked it there, then completed the circuit by returning to the first end.

"Now, it's Addie's turn, since she got a lot of things started by being born here on the Slash-C."

The little girl applied serious concentration to her task, and with a little assist from Val on one end and Jack at the other, did it perfectly.

"Then Jack," Ed said. "Though truth to tell, he should be last, considering how stubborn he was when all the rest of us knew how things were."

Chuckles came at that.

"Now, Val and Jack have asked a few more folks to thread a strand. Donna and me. Eleanor and Cahill, Matty and Dave. Cal and Taylor. Lucy and Jimmy, Valerie's parents. Dax and Kiernan." As he called their names, they came up and added strands. "What I think they're saying is we all contributed to their coming together. Some might call it meddling, but I prefer *contributed to*."

That drew more chuckles.

"Now that all the strands are in place, Val, you start turning your end, and that will twist each group of strands together, so we end up with three lengths."

As Val cranked with enthusiasm the audience leaned forward, a few saying, "Look at that."

"Good job, Val. Okay, Jack, you're going to start cranking smooth and steady, while Val goes a little slower on her end. But first, Addie and I are going to set this guide stick in here to keep those nicely twisted strands from getting knotted up. That's right, Addie. I'll put my hand over yours so nothing can scratch you and now Jack and Val, you go ahead and start cranking."

Almost immediately, the strands began to come together, forming a recognizable rope, which grew longer as Addie—under Ed's direction and protection—moved steadily from Val's end to Jack's end.

With a few deft motions, Ed released and prepared the ends, added a knot at one end, then slid the other through a hondo, turning the line of the rope into a circle.

"We started out with a few individual strings. Through teamwork, cooperation, and a little bit of old-fashioned ingenuity, Jack and Val and Addie have made a rope. Now that rope's a loop. To remind them they're all in this together and there's no beginning or end to loving each other."

"Shhh."

For a second Ethan thought Hannah's quiet sound was directed at the thoughts rumbling and crashing in his head.

Good luck with that.

Then he realized she'd directed it at Sarah, sitting on the other side of Mandy.

Sarah leaned forward to look past Mandy at him and grin naughtily. He smiled back automatically.

"Ethan," Mandy scolded in a low voice. "Don't encour—"

She broke it off, staring at him.

As if she knew.

Worse, words she'd spoken to him this morning roared through his head even louder than the other ones.

…you keep yourself and Paige and everybody else on a schedule as if one small change will let everything fall apart…

Past Sarah, he could see Chal now sitting on Hannah's lap, small fingers playing with the point of her collar as he leaned against her, his eyes drifting closed.

…everybody needs more than common sense, Ethan. They need to know that their needs, sometimes even their wants, come before a schedule…

Sarah waved to him.

Hannah put a hand over her daughter's. She started to look up, but before her eyes would meet his, he sat back, still avoiding Mandy's gaze.

Paige's voice came then. Softer, gentler, yet heard so clearly over all the other thoughts in his head.

I love you. I have always loved you. I always will love you. …. I'm having your baby, Ethan Chalmers, and I refuse to be anything but ecstatic about it.

There would be a new life. One that they had created together.

A baby. Becoming a person as distinct, as individual as Sarah, as Chal.

Their child, his and Paige's. The result of a love that kept the universe in order.

Then Mandy was back—had to have the final word, of course.

Forget your schedule for a minute and feel, Ethan. You've been so busy protecting against the bad stuff you're not letting yourself feel the good stuff.

"You may kiss the bride."

Jack didn't take Reverend Foley up on his offer right away. He held the moment, looking into her eyes, a smile coming slowly, then spreading wider and wider. She smiled right back at him.

So when he bent to kiss her, hands on either side of her face, and she threw her arms around his neck, they kissed and kissed again and then a third time, all while smiling.

They looked at each other a moment longer, then Jack raised one arm in triumph to those gathered, who cheered in response.

He picked up Addie, swinging her onto a shoulder, then wrapped the other arm around Val and, as Cahill struck up a joyful, energetic tune, they started back down the twisty aisle together.

CHAPTER TWENTY-TWO

Ethan turned to her, holding on to her hand to keep her seated when she would have stood to join the other guests flowing toward the back.

"We need to talk."

He didn't have to hold her to keep her seated now. "We both need some time—"

Mandy, standing, bumped against his knees. "C'mon, what's the hold up?"

"Go away, Mandy." He glanced past her. "Kiernan's gone to back up Cahill. Go that way. Paige, we need to talk. Now."

"Not now. This isn't—"

"Yes, now. It's important. The most impor—"

"Oh, my God. You're finally telling her she's more important than your master schedule? But *now*? *Here*? Like *this*?" Mandy demanded.

"If I had a chance—" he started.

"What's the holdup?" Hannah asked from down the row.

"Ethan is asking Paige to marry him sooner than The Plan dictates," Mandy said over her shoulder.

"Here? Now?" Hannah asked.

Ethan stood, holding on to Paige's hand. "Now, yes. But not here. C'mon, Paige. Let's find someplace quiet."

Cahill, with Kiernan on the second guitar, played the same, almost restrained, tune Dave had identified as "Haste to the Wedding." But now it grew and grew, leaving sedate far behind and becoming recognizable as a jig.

The upbeat tempo got even the slowest of the guests on their feet and moving through the aisles to the open area behind the hay bales, where what might have started as a reception line had evolved into a hugfest.

Music from speakers picked up the same jig Cahill had been playing—though even faster and with many more instruments, including hard-driving drums—freeing him to pull his brother by the arm to join the group. He circled an arm around his wife and began moving to the music.

Val picked it up, bouncing up and down on her toes, with her bouquet held aloft.

Everyone soon joined in to some degree or another, with a couple doing a fair rendition of a jig, and laughs and smiles all around.

Even the photographer/videographer, who'd been trying to round up the wedding party for photos, gave up, grinning and dancing a bit herself as she shot the celebration.

With the triumphant end of the song, a cheer rose from all. Then El took Val firmly by the arm and headed her back toward the altar for photos, while Donna guided the guests toward the patio.

On the far side of the barn, with no one but a few horses as observers, he swung around to face her. "Marry me, Paige."

"Our plan—"

"No, not according to our plan."

She touched his face softly. "I know it's not according to our plan. I—"

"That's not what I mean—"

"—know you planned carefully and your plan makes so much sense, it's so practical. But a baby… I know this—"

"Paige."

"—will delay reaching our goals for the right house and we won't have as big a nest egg before we start a family the way we planned, but—"

"Screw the plan."

She blinked at him.

"Screw the whole thing. That's what I'm saying. Marry me now, Paige. Not later according to some stupid schedule. Marry me now."

"Ethan, we don't need to make this decision this minute." She said it soothingly, like she thought she might be talking to a lunatic. "We just found out. All the emotions—We can give it time. Think things through. Make the best decision after we've thought it through. I know you need—"

"I need you. That's what I need. First, last, and always, I need you. And now—" He had to swallow to say it. "—our baby."

"Ethan—"

He knew she was going to talk sense to him. Probably plans and schedules, too.

He kissed her.

He felt her uncertainty for a moment. He didn't push. He kept kissing her.

Hoping it expressed his heart.

Hoping it trumped all those earlier words he'd spoken.

Hoping she knew him as well as he'd always been so sure she did.

She gave a little *ah* into his mouth and he felt her uncertainty melt.

After dinner, then the ceremonial cutting and enjoyable eating of the wedding brownies, Dave stood and called for attention.

"Jack and Val had some very specific things they said no to about this wedding. For example, we know they said no presents, but—"

"No. Absolutely not." Val shook her head. "And you've all already done so much for us, with the quilts and the tables and the plates and—"

"Tomorrow's brunch," called out Hugh Moski. "Don't forget that."

"Shush," his wife, Ruth, said. "You're not supposed to be on her side."

"Wait a minute," Dave ordered. "Let me finish. Because this isn't a present for you two."

That stopped Val and got her interest.

"Shane? Cal?"

At Dave's invitation, each man came up and placed two large buckets in front of the bride and groom.

They were filled with cash.

"This is for the horses Jack helps. Especially the ones who can't get to the point where they can go to regular folks. Consider it a sort of scholarship fund. To help them here, and then to send the ones that don't graduate on to Matt's retirement home for old and unrideable horses."

Jack grinned, while Val's mouth dropped.

"But how on earth—? This is a fortune. How did you—? Where did it all come from?"

"Hah," Hugh Moski crowed, "we surprised 'em but good."

"We've had jars out around town since last summer," Ruth said. "We knew this day would come sooner than you did. Had 'em all over. Doc's and Taylor's office. The library, even though that wasn't official, and especially the café—"

"Rainie, you did? I was in there all the time. I never saw it."

"That's a miracle, because we had to keep hiding it when you came around, Val. You almost caught us a dozen times. And some of the school kids did a car wash to raise funds, not to mention Lisa had a jar in her studio."

That started a spate of stories about how Valerie or Jack or both had nearly spotted one of the jars.

Dave reined it in by whistling into the microphone.

"I strongly suspect the next prohibition they put on this wedding was to keep me from making a speech—"

"Yet, there you are, giving a speech," Lisa called out in sisterly teasing.

"—and telling tales on Jack," he added firmly when the laughter died down. "So, instead of speeches, Irene and Ted Weston brought us another way for each of us here to express our good wishes. Dax?"

Dax got up and went to the canvas covered doors with the hooks.

"Dad looked in to this and we can attach this to the side of your house by the door, so you'll be reminded each time you go in or out—"

"Let them see it before you get into the engineering, Dave," Matty said. "Then they'll understand."

"Okay, okay."

Dax took one bottom corner of the canvas, Dave got the other and they lifted.

"This is to wish you both as much luck as we can."

The wooden door was now covered with individual horseshoes held by the hooks Val had seen earlier. Old horseshoes, new horseshoes, each with something written in indelible pen.

"Each guest brought a horseshoe and wrote a wish on it for you," Dave said.

Val and Jack were up now, looking at the horseshoes, reading some of the wishes and names.

"Some of us needed help getting horseshoes," called out Anthony. "So thanks to the Wyoming folks for covering us."

"Oh, oh," was all Val could get out.

"You'll have plenty of time to read them all later. And with Dad's idea of how to hang this, you can take a look at a few any time you're sitting on your porch. For right now, we'll just say we wish you both—you all—every happiness there is. Lift your glasses everyone—to Jack and Valerie."

"And me!" came a firm voice.

"And Addie," Dave added solemnly, as everyone toasted the new family.

CHAPTER TWENTY-THREE

"We've been promised some line dancing," Cahill said into the microphone, and there was a combination cheer and groan from those gathered, "but before we do, we need the bride and groom up here for their first dance together."

That quieted the group.

Jack led Val onto the dance floor created when most of the tables and chairs were packed away after dinner.

As Cahill sang and played a haunting and sweet song about the wish to grow old together and all that would bring, Jack and Val danced, looking into each other's faces with smiles that had their guests smiling as well … along with a few tears.

But as the song seemed destined to fade sweetly away, Cahill set up a new rhythm by drumming and slapping his guitar. In an instant, Kiernan joined in on a second guitar, and then Cahill led as they both took off on a fast trip on the Irish song "Road to Lisdoonvarna." Likely not many in the group knew the song, but they all felt the rhythm.

Grinning, Val lifted her skirts and Jack came beside her. Addie and Brennan ran onto the dance floor and stopped in front of them, mimicking the positions of the wedding couple, then all four of them began an entirely original dance, which blended line dancing, jig, and square dancing, with a dash of who-the-heck-knows thrown in.

The audience was stomping and clapping in time, when they weren't laughing too hard.

At the end, calls of "encore, encore" made them do it all over again.

Until the dancers were so breathless that Addie, followed by Brennan, sat down for the last few bars and Val sagged against Jack.

With the applause still sounding and Cahill giving way to a local teen who loved to DJ, Val drew her parents into the center, while Jack went to get Donna and Ed. The six of them met in a sort of swaying group hug to the start of the Rascal Flatts song about wishing that the life of someone you love will become all that it can be. The three couples danced, switching off partners, until they met again at the end in another swaying group hug.

"*Alllll riiight*," called out the young DJ, "let's see some of this line dancing I've been hearing about!"

As the night darkened, campfires were lit some distance from the patio, for those who chose to talk away from the line dancing music. Set back from the enclosed fires, the hay bales added more seating.

Watchers were assigned to each, both to keep the fires going and to make sure none of the kids chasing fireflies came too close.

Val and Jack moved easily among their guests. Mostly together, occasionally splitting up to cover more territory.

Jack came up to her after one of those brief apart times, putting his arm around her shoulders. "You look pretty serious for someone who just got married."

She smiled up at him, but the smile faltered when she said, "I was watching Kiernan. He's so hurt. And sad. And you didn't make it any easier on him by having him take her to the airport. Why on earth did you do that?"

"Figured it was harder short-term, easier long-term. Better to shake him up now than let him slide in too deep. Especially since he can't count on finding someone who'd drag him out of his hole. Not since I've snapped up the best one."

Val blinked. "Oh. You did it to make him face up to things right away."

He nodded. "I know what comes of packing down those feelings to where they fester and poison, until they paralyze you. Better he learns from my mistakes and faces it early."

She stretched up and kissed him on the cheek. "You are an old softy, Jack Ralston. Just like with your horses. But Kiernan isn't a horse. You have another method to reach him. He understands words."

"Val—"

"Go talk to him."

"We can do that."

"Not *we. You.* He needs to hear it from you."

"Well, if I'm going alone it has to wait until after we dance again. They're finally playing a slow one."

Nudged by his bride as the last notes of the song played, Jack found Kiernan sitting on the farthest hay bale by the farthest fire.

He put a hand on Kiernan's shoulder as he sat beside him. "You willing to forgive me?"

The younger man's mouth twisted. "*Me* forgive *you?*"

"For that airport run. It was a hell of request, as my bride has mentioned."

"It was the least I could do for you and Val."

"You got that wrong. It was the least you could do for yourself." He considered that a moment. "Maybe for Felicity, too."

"I don't know how I didn't see what she—"

"Doesn't matter now, Kiernan. What matters is what you see, what you do, from this point on. Kicking yourself for the past doesn't change it. Got any doubts about that, look at me as a shining example of going about it the wrong way. Only when I got a few, uh, pointers on that from Val and accepted the truth of it did I start seeing I had a future. A future with Val and Addie and the rest of our family."

"There should be only joy for you—"

"There is. Don't you worry about Val and me. We're fine." A grin spread across his face. "Better than fine. We're married."

The DJ had long ago packed up and left, yawning mightily.

But most of the guests remained.

The children were asleep in the main house, lined up on the floors in sleeping bags, "Like orderly cocoons, who'll burst out in the morning with enough energy to send rockets to the moon," according to Dave.

A few of the adults still danced, though slow songs dominated now.

Occasionally the music was provided by the groups around the campfires, as an old favorite would start with one group, then be picked up by another and another.

Gradually, the eastern sky lightened.

SUNDAY
Brunch

Neighbors and friends from Knighton swooped in—some having only left an hour or so earlier, while guests from farther away stayed on—bringing the makings for brunch, as well as already baked goods.

Everyone lingered well after the meal, giving the bride and groom more time to sit and talk with the guests.

Jack stored up every story about Val he heard from the chef she'd worked for, her colleague from the radio station, the friends she had since childhood, the cousins who'd known her from birth, the woman who'd worked with her and Eleanor at The Fishwife, then taken it over.

As she had at that first dinner, Val looked around at friends and family connecting.

Shane Garrison's parents were talking with Walker and Kalli Riley and the Vances—Thomas, his wife, Judi, and his half-sister, Becky. Jack had gotten to know Thomas when he first came to Wyoming.

Her brothers were with the Ruskoffs, Doc Johnson, Ethan, Paige, and a local rancher named Conner Malloy. Her dad, Ted Weston, Manuela Ruiz, and the chef were in deep conversation. Her mother and the Widow Brontman appeared to be trading recipes. Her friends from Gloucester and her cousins were with Lisa, Shane, Taylor's brother, Hannah, and Dax.

But that was just a snapshot, because the combinations shifted, merged, reformed.

But then began the bittersweet farewells.

The Trimarco clan, along with Eleanor, Cahill, and Kiernan would stay another couple days, while Lisa and Shane, plus Taylor's relatives, would stay on for another week. But many of the rest were scattering to airports, car trips, or their homes.

Her cousins were headed to Yellowstone, as was her colleague from the radio station. Her former chef boss was going to Denver. Manuela was heading straight back to The Fishwife.

Walker and Kalli Riley and their kids left with Matt Halderman and Zoe Parisi. The Rileys would be back in Park to run the next night's rodeo.

The Vances, Jack's friends from southeastern Wyoming, promised to come again and invited them to come visit their horse ranch.

Then it was time for the Bardville group to go.

"Boone, thank you again for getting the houses all done, so we could have everybody here," Val said.

He chuckled. "You've thanked me at least three times, Jack and Matty a couple times each, Donna and Ed and the Trimarcos, and Cahill and Eleanor, and I think a couple of the little ones have said it, too. But it was all my workers. I only came to check on them the once."

"They were absolutely great," Val agreed. "But you were the one who sent them here."

"And you would have been welcome to come as many times as you wanted," Matty said.

"No, no, no," objected Cambria with a laugh. "He's still working on letting go. Don't encourage him to regress."

"Then come back now that they're done," Matty responded triumphantly. "All of you. Any of you. Whenever you can."

"Sorry to say, it's time," Ted said.

They were hugging and hugging, making sure each hugged all of the others.

At the end, Donna hugged Paige, pushing the hair back from her face.

"Oh," said Lisa, "Now you're in trouble. She's treating you like one of her kids."

"I'm honored," Paige said with tears in her eyes.

"Good thing," Ed said, "because Donna's already looking at side trips to North Carolina."

"Oh, that would be wonderful," Mandy said. "Please do."

"Once you're driving from Wyoming to New York, North Carolina doesn't seems too far," Donna said. "Especially if there's a special reason."

Paige colored, but nothing more was said that Val heard, except when Donna said softly to Ethan, "Take good care of her. I understand you were given some advice about a plant?"

He jolted, then said slowly, "Trillium."

She nodded.

Then they were all in the vehicles and pulling away, while those remaining waved them off.

"Donna?"

"Yes, Valerie?"

There was something in the older woman's eyes that made Val shy away from asking her directly about the plant and the Flower Power woman. Instead, she asked, "Was it my family and all of you getting to know each other you were thinking about last week when you talked about weddings bringing people together? About Paige and Ethan? Or—" She turned to the older woman. "—was it Felicity coming."

Donna's eyebrows popped up. "Now, how on earth would I have known about that? No, no, it was general musing, that's all."

"Sorry. Maybe my imagination was getting away from me."

"It certainly was. After all, it's not like I'm the Flower Power woman."

Donna grinned as she watched looks zing around the group at that. Looks among the men, looks among the women.

Then she saw Ed watching her.

He shook his head slightly, put one arm around her, and leaned in close. "What are you up to now?"

She stretched up to kiss him on the cheek. He didn't seem to require any further answer.

Later that afternoon, the bride and groom made a point to sit down with their daughter, feeling they might have neglected her during this hectic time.

But Addie cut the time short, eager to get back to showing Brennan that she could too throw a child's practice rope as good as him.

Jack spent time with DMC, while Val watched from the rise behind the corral. When he was done, he walked up to join her. They sat together, watching the sun set.

And then they went to bed, with the twilight still strong and the fireflies starting to flash.

"You told her *what?*" his bride demanded of him.

Jack offered her another cracker and the knife for digging in the peanut butter jar. She declined both. Instead, she twirled her hand, indicating he was to repeat what he'd said.

So he did.

"And then I told her she was kidding herself about not caring for Kiernan."

She flopped back to the pillows. "What am I going to do with you, Jack Ralston?"

"I have some suggestions."

"Never mind that now," she said sternly. "You should have been tearing that girl up one side and down the other for what she did."

Her sternness lost some effectiveness when she popped back up and dug into the peanut butter.

"Yeah? What about you?" He swiped a smudge from the corner of her mouth with the side of his thumb.

"What about me?"

"Don't go all brown-eyed innocence on me. I know better." He stroked her and she giggled. "Heard about you going to see Felicity this morning."

"How did you—"

"Donna was there. Helping her pack, according to Donna. But apparently she'd been saying a few things to Felicity, too, only you came in and left her in your dust." He went solemn. "She told me what you said about keeping Hayley alive in our hearts." He kissed her forehead. "Thank you for that."

She cleared her throat and nodded. "But as for Kiernan, even if Felicity realizes—decides—she truly cares about him and that's why she kept seeing him… He might not ever believe it."

He looked over at her. "You're right. But *she* needs to be honest with herself about it. And whatever you say about me trying to help her or butting in where it's none of my business—What? What are you laughing about?"

"You. Me. Us. Not to mention Donna and the rest of the Slash-C folks playing Cupid for Ethan and Paige…"

"Cupid? They were already a couple."

After she explained, he kissed her. Kissed her again.

Then he pushed knife, peanut butter, and crackers onto the floor. And there wasn't any more talking for a long while.

Afterward, Val turned in Jack's arms. "This was the best wedding ever."

He kissed her, then said, "Just wait for the honeymoon."

She grinned at him. "Just wait for all the years to come after."

If you enjoyed A Cowboy Wedding, I hope you'll consider leaving a review, to let your fellow readers know about your experience.

For news about upcoming books, subscribe to Patricia McLinn's free newsletter here:

www.patriciamclinn.com/readers-list

Dear Readers,

First, if you'd like to hear the songs from Val and Jack's wedding, there's a playlist on my website on the A Cowboy Wedding page—www.patriciamclinn.com/book/a-cowboy-wedding. Enjoy!

The characters usually tell me loud and clear what's going to happen, but this time Kiernan is being stubborn (*Men*! And especially *Irish men*!)

So I'd love to hear what you think—can Kiernan and Felicity make a match of it after all? Or should Kiernan find a new love?

Just email your thoughts to patriciamclinnauthor@gmail.com with the subject "Kiernan."

Looking forward to reading your thoughts!

Patricia McLinn

The Wyoming Wildflowers series

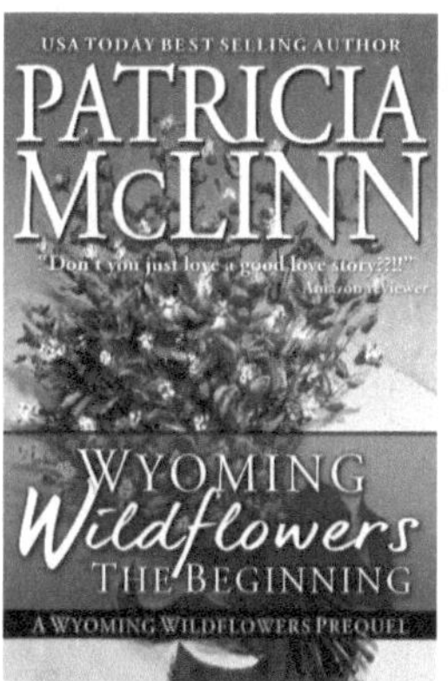

Donna and Ed's lives are worlds apart. Can they ever bridge
the distance…

Wyoming Wildflowers: The Beginning

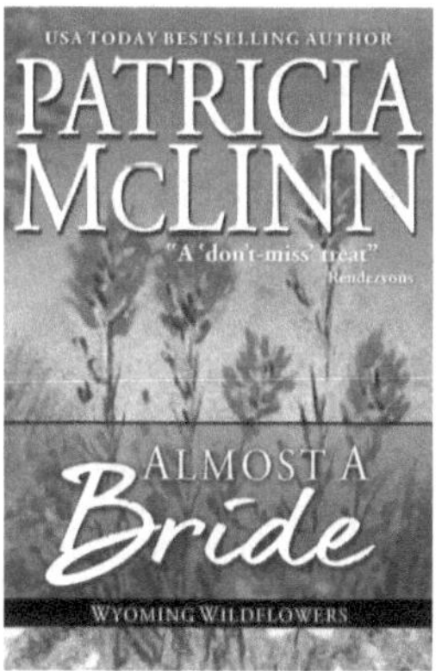

Dave Currick has everything he wants, except the woman he loves…

Almost a Bride

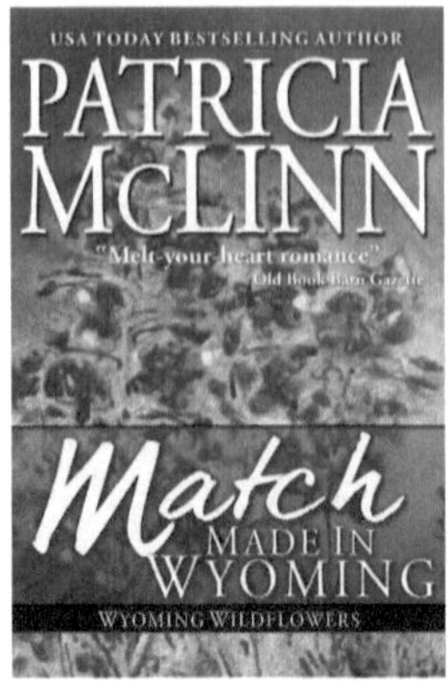

Cal and Taylor can spark a wildfire, but will they come together in…
Match Made in Wyoming

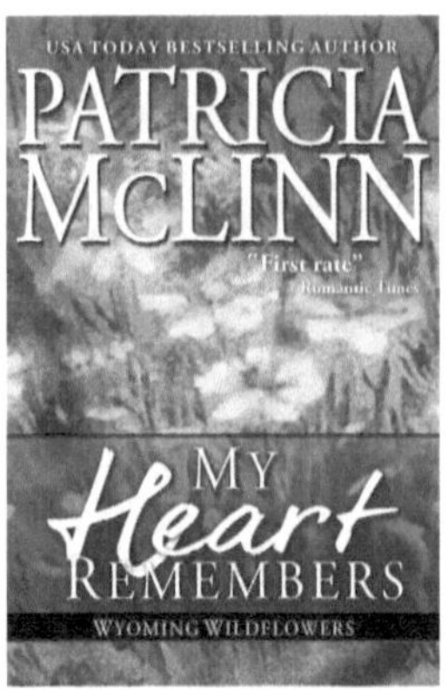

Lisa's carried a secret in her heart for years—and he just hit town…
My Heart Remembers

Prequel to Jack's Heart
A New World

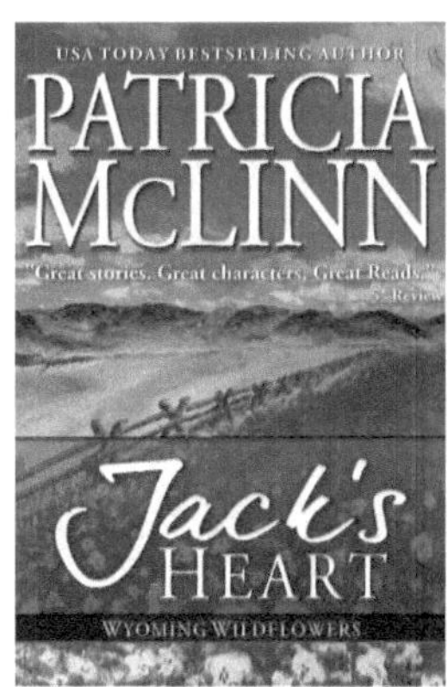

New England single mom meets her Lone Ranger.
Jack's Heart

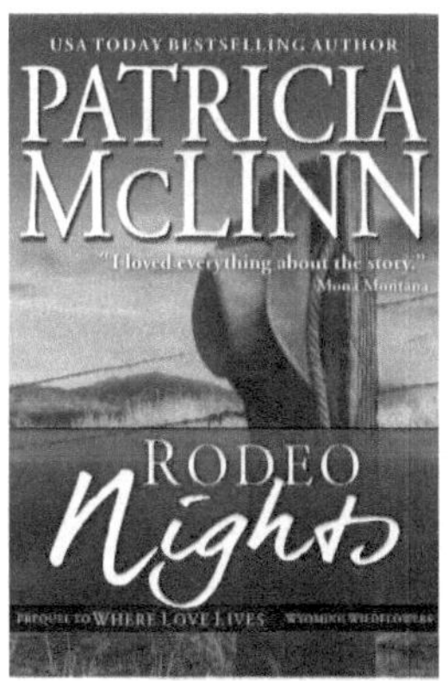

Prequel to Where Love Lives
Rodeo Nights

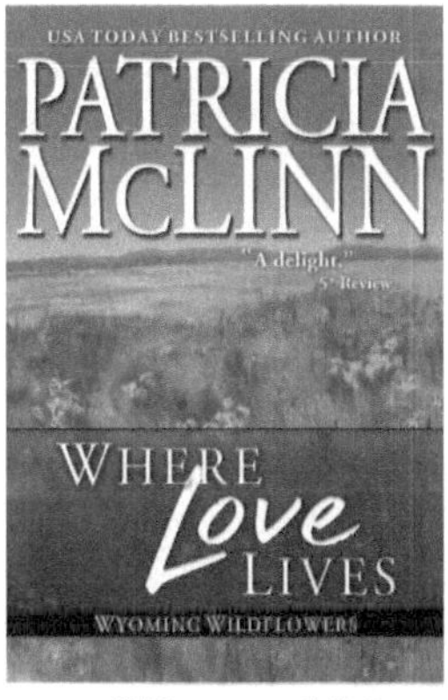

One night stands in the way of Zoe and Matt spending the rest of their days together.
Where Love Lives

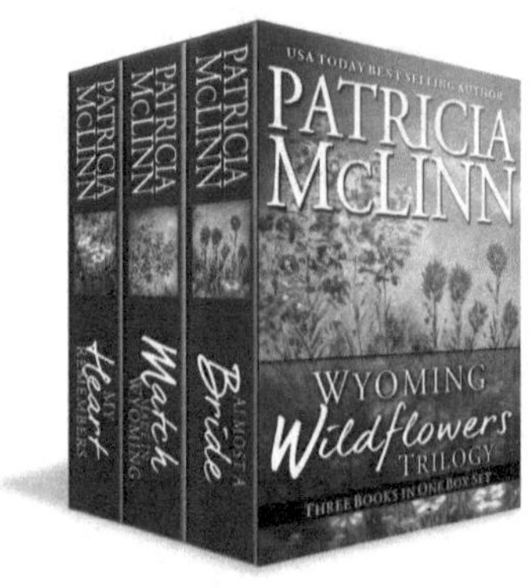

Read three books for one great price in the Wyoming Wildflowers boxed set…

Wyoming Wildflowers Trilogy (Books 2–4)

If you like western romances, try these other Patricia McLinn series:

The Bardville, Wyoming series

A Place Called Home series

And the stand-alone Ride the River: Rodeo Knights

For more about the contemporary romance series connected to A Cowboy Wedding, check out:

The Wedding Series

patriciamclinn.com/patricias-books/romances/the-wedding-series

Discover more of Patricia's books at
www.patriciamclinn.com/patricias-books

Or get a printable booklist
www.patriciamclinn.com/patricias-books/printable-booklist

About the Author

USA Today bestselling author Patricia McLinn's novels—cited by reviewers for warmth, wit and vivid characterization—have won numerous regional and national awards and been on national bestseller lists.

In addition to her romance and women's fiction books, Patricia is the author of the Caught Dead in Wyoming mystery series, which adds a touch of humor and romance to figuring out whodunit.

Patricia received BA and MSJ degrees from Northwestern University. She was a sports writer (Rockford, Ill.), assistant sports editor (Charlotte, N.C.) and—for 20-plus years—an editor at The Washington Post. She has spoken about writing from Melbourne, Australia to Washington, D.C., including being a guest-speaker at the Smithsonian Institution.

She is now living in Northern Kentucky, and writing full-time. Patricia loves to hear from readers through her website, Facebook and Twitter.

Visit with Patricia:

Website: https://www.patriciamclinn.com

Facebook: facebook.com/PatriciaMcLinn

Twitter: @PatriciaMcLinn

Pinterest: pinterest.com/patriciamclinn

Copyright © Patricia McLinn
ISBN: 978-1-944126-13-1

www.ingramcontent.com/pod-product-compliance
Lightning Source LLC
Chambersburg PA
CBHW050407190726
48284CB00007BB/2471